Pride Publishing books by Ann Marie James

Everyone's Mechanic
Chasing the Dream
Fearing the Dream
Resisting the Dream

Kingdom of Corazón
The Way to a Man's Heart

I0544802

Everyone's Mechanic

RESISTING THE DREAM

ANN MARIE JAMES

Resisting the Dream
ISBN # 978-1-83943-738-0
©Copyright Ann Marie James 2021
Cover Art by Erin Dameron-Hill ©Copyright September 2021
Interior text design by Claire Siemaszkiewicz
Pride Publishing

Published in 2021 by Pride Publishing, United Kingdom.

Pride Publishing is an imprint of Totally Entwined Group Limited.

RESISTING THE DREAM

Dedication

As always, a huge thank you goes to my family.

Chapter One

Nikolai Barinov tore his gaze away from the numbers on his computer screen to check who'd just come in the entrance to Everyone's Mechanic. His professional smile changed to a genuine one when he saw his cousin Sergei standing in front of him.

"Hello, Nikolai. How's my favorite cousin?"

"Uh-oh. You only call me your favorite cousin when you want something."

Sergei placed a hand on his chest. "I'm wounded."

Nikolai raised one blond eyebrow at Sergei, then sat back and waited. The smile fell from Sergei's mouth.

"What happened to your face?"

"What?" *Shit, can he see the bruise? I thought the makeup covered it.*

"You have a bruise on your cheek. What the hell happened?"

"Would you believe I ran into a door?"

Sergei widened his stance and put his hands on his hips, giving Nikolai his sternest stare. Nikolai rushed to explain. "Seriously, I saw Brandon going into your building yesterday afternoon as I was leaving, and I was so busy watching him that I ran right into the doorjamb." Nikolai grimaced. "Not my finest moment, to be sure."

Sergei's stern expression morphed into an amused one and he coughed into his hand while avoiding eye contact with Nikolai. When their gazes met, Sergei lost the fight and laughed until he had tears running down his face and had to lean against the counter to support himself.

Nikolai shook his head in disgust at his cousin's antics. "Yeah, yeah. Laugh it up. You do realize you probably just got grease on your suit, right?" Working at a garage had its advantages, including the apartment he was able to rent above the business, but spic and span cleanliness was not one of those perks. Oh, the owner, Kirk, ran a tight ship and everything was as clean as possible, but it was still a garage. It was Nikolai's turn to laugh as Sergei looked down at himself to search for dirt on his custom suit.

Sergei took a swipe at his jacket before shrugging and looking back at Nikolai.

"So, why are you here?"

"I need a favor."

"I figured." Nikolai made a rolling hand gesture to try to encourage Sergei to spit it out.

Sergei's forehead furrowed. "I'm a little concerned, though, that you won't be able to complete this favor without causing yourself bodily harm."

"What? Why?"

"I need you to work with Brandon on a project."

"You need me to work with your personal assistant, Brandon Whitaker, on a project? But he hates me."

"He doesn't hate you."

"Doesn't know what to do with me then?"

Sergei shrugged one of his massive shoulders as Nikolai wished for the thousandth time that he had gotten some of Sergei's six-foot-plus height and size. Alas, he was stuck at a measly, svelte five-foot-seven. "I can't deny that. You confuse him, for sure, but he does respect you. He loves the reports you set up for him while you were interning last summer."

"He was shocked I could even do spreadsheets and reports, though. He thinks I'm an idiot."

"Only because you turn into a nervous klutz whenever he is around. A doorjamb? Really?"

"What? There's something about him that does it for me — brown hair, brown eyes, six feet tall, those broad shoulders... Yum. What's not to love? I know intellectually that nothing will ever come of it. Have you seen the women who come to meet him for lunch?"

"Yes, I have, and I also know none of them last more than a month."

"He's not gay. The number of women he takes out makes that very clear."

"I don't think he's as straight as he pretends to be."

"What do you mean?"

"I mean he watches you when you aren't looking."

Nikolai waved his hand in the air. "He's just trying to figure me out. As you said, I confuse him. He's not a man who likes to be confused. He's the man with a plan for everything."

"Exactly my point — and I don't think he planned for you."

"Whatever. What is it you needed me to work on with Brandon?"

"I would like you guys to work on plans for an LGBTQ center — a place where teens can come to either hang out or to get help, counseling, the whole nine yards. I want to offer classes as well — financial ones like budgeting and checkbook balancing as well as cooking and other basics. Maybe you can talk to some of the instructors at that dojo you go to and see if they would teach some self-defense classes too. The statistics for homeless youth — especially gay homeless youth — are scary, and I want to do something about it. It will be open to all but mainly to support the community."

Nikolai was getting excited about the project. The center was something that was desperately needed there in Raleigh and elsewhere. He felt a slight twinge at Sergei's casual dismissal of his time spent at the dojo. He wasn't sure what his family thought he did there three-to-five days a week, but obviously it wasn't learning any of the skills they taught, but that was partly his fault as he'd never told them when he'd received his different color belts. It was something private for him.

He was snapped out of his ponderings by the ding of the door sensor as someone else came in. He opened his eyes wide when he realized it was Brandon. He went to stand, the chair slipped back too fast and he almost fell, catching himself with a hand on the desk, just in time. Nikolai flushed with mortification as his cheeks got hot and he ducked his head, pretending to search for something on his desk in a sad attempt to seem like he had everything under control. Snagging a pencil, Nikolai pulled his long, wavy blond hair up in a messy bun on top of his head, and shoved the pencil in to secure it.

He glanced up after a moment to find Sergei staring at him in exasperation then turning to greet Brandon. "Hey, Brandon, thanks for giving me a minute with Nikolai before coming in. Nikolai is really excited about the project."

Nikolai took a deep breath to compose himself then turned to face Brandon. "Nice to see you again, Brandon. This should be an interesting project. I look forward to working with you on it." *There. That wasn't too psycho.*

"Yeah. It will be a challenge, but I think we can come up with something great. I know you're pretty busy with school and here, so when do you think we can meet to get started?"

"Well, I've already successfully defended my thesis, so my load at school is pretty light. I'm just waiting on graduation now."

Sergei's gaze snapped back to Nikolai. "Wait! When did that happen?"

"A couple of weeks ago," Nikolai said with a shrug.

"Why didn't you say anything? We should have celebrated."

"Well, first you were in London at that big conference, then you hibernated with your hubby for the weekend and didn't come to family dinner. It just kind of got lost in the shuffle."

"Did your family go to your thesis defense, at least?" Sergei asked, frowning.

Nikolai couldn't quite hide his grimace. "Um, your parents and Sasha came. My parents couldn't make it. It wasn't a big deal." Nikolai didn't even believe himself, so he knew Sergei didn't.

"We'll discuss this later."

"Nothing to discuss."

Sergei scowled at him. "There's a lot to discuss, but first, do you definitely want in on this project?"

"Of course, I'm in. It's important."

"Agreed. So, when are you available to meet on it?"

"I have sessions at the dojo tonight and tomorrow morning, but I'm free after that. I know tomorrow's Saturday, so we can postpone to next week if you guys need to."

"Saturday afternoon works for me. What about you Brandon?"

"Yep. That works. I have somewhere to be in the morning as well, but I will be free about noon."

"Great. How about we meet at my house then? I'll feed you all lunch."

"Sounds good," Brandon and Nikolai answered together. Nikolai could only shake his head at himself after the bolt of arousal that went through his system when he made brief eye contact with Brandon's brown-eyed gaze. He hazarded a small smile at the man, but Brandon didn't respond, instead breaking the connection and turning toward Sergei. "Okay. Glad that's settled. We need to get moving. We have that meeting at two o'clock with the planning commissioner about your new property on Fayette Street." Brandon then turned and walked out of the door after a head nod to Nikolai.

"Plan to stay after the meeting to continue our discussion about your thesis defense."

"It really wasn't a big deal, Sergei. You know my family doesn't understand or approve of me and my ways." Nikolai put air quotes around the 'my ways', as it was a common phrase from his mother. His mother and father were not the warm and supportive parents that Sergei's were. Nikolai's father was very much about toxic masculinity and a woman knowing her place in the world. Nikolai did not fit his father's definition of a good son at all, so he was ignored — and that was fine with him. It really was, but Sergei never understood, mainly because Nikolai's father was always on his best behavior whenever Sergei was around, thinking he could use his connection with Sergei for his own needs in some way.

The truth was — and one his father would never admit — that Nikolai's father was both scared and jealous in equal parts of Sergei's power. He felt that as the older Barinov male, he should have been the one to have the influence and wealth that Sergei had accumulated and that Sergei should seek his council like he was smarter, because of his age. Sergei was actually one of the most intelligent people Nikolai knew, and that was saying something because Nikolai had been going to school forever.

Sergei was also one of the hardest-working people he knew, with Brandon being right up there with him. Brandon was truly Sergei's right-hand man, and Nikolai wasn't saying that because he had a major crush on the man either. Part of the reason he had such a crush on him was because he worked so hard and was so dedicated to Sergei. Nikolai's father was lazy and dedicated only to himself. *Sad, but true.*

Sergei interrupted his thoughts, and Nikolai scrambled to remember what they were talking about. "Not. The. Point. I don't care how your parents feel about things. This is about communication between you and me. We will discuss it Saturday. Da?"

"Da, Sergei," Nikolai conceded grudgingly.

"Good. I will see you tomorrow." Sergei then followed Brandon out of the door.

Chapter Two

Brandon made it to the car and got behind the wheel to wait for Sergei. He was glad Sergei had stayed behind to continue his conversation with Nikolai. He needed a moment. The jolt that had gone through him when they'd made eye contact had rattled him. He didn't know what to do with his attraction to Nikolai. That hadn't been the plan. Oh, he knew he was gay, but he didn't have time to date right now. Dating wasn't on the schedule until he was thirty-one.

The women he took to lunch or dinner occasionally didn't count. He wasn't really dating them, no matter what everyone thought. It had started out as a way for him to cover the fact he was gay when he'd first started working for Sergei, before he'd realized his boss was bisexual. The first time he'd seen Sergei with a male date had shocked Brandon, but Sergei didn't care what anyone thought of him. He was who he was, and no one would dare say anything to him about it—but he didn't have that level of self- confidence.

Brandon banged his head against the steering wheel a few times but stopped when the passenger door suddenly opened. He sat back in his seat and tightened his grip on the steering wheel before turning his head to look at Sergei, only to startle when he found Sergei staring right at him.

"What?"

"Why do you dislike Nikolai so much?"

"I don't dislike Nikolai. He's a great guy."

"Could have fooled me. You act like he has some horrible disease and smells bad every time you speak to him."

"I don't mean to. He's just so…" Brandon trailed off and waved his hands in the air, not sure how he wanted to finish that sentence.

Sergei's voice hardened and his Russian accent thickened as it only did when he was upset. "Gay? Do you have a problem with him being gay? Or me being bi, for that matter?"

"No! Of course not! *I'm* gay!" Brandon realized he was yelling and lowered his voice. "I'm gay."

"I thought so. Then why?"

"Because he could be everything to me, and I can't deal with that right now."

"Why not?"

Brandon stared at his hands where he flexed his fingers on the steering wheel rather than meet his boss' stare. "After I graduated from college with my bachelor's and was hired on full-time at your company, I sued my mother for custody of my little brother, Jeremy. She has an addiction problem. I didn't want my brother to grow up like I did. I wanted him to know there would always be food on the table and a roof over his head."

The tone of Sergei's voice changed. "How old is he, and why is this the first I've heard of him?"

"Jeremy is fifteen now. He was ten when I first got custody of him. I didn't tell you at first because I was scared you would think I couldn't do the job because I have a kid, especially as I was using the company education reimbursement program to pay for my MBA, then I didn't know how to bring it up."

"I can understand why you thought that. Was it hard getting custody?"

Brandon snorted. "Not after my mother showed up to court high on something and reeking of alcohol. The judge was *not* impressed. She signed over her rights right then, and I was eventually allowed to adopt him." Brandon didn't mention the two years of anxiety and home visits before the courts had decided that Jeremy could stay and the adoption had been finalized. He had gone to college on a scholarship and had worked hard to impress during his internship at Sergei's company. He had steadily worked his way up in the ranks after graduation until he was now Sergei's assistant...his go-to guy. He couldn't take his eye off the prize now. He had no time for distraction.

"I've worked so hard for so long to get where I am and make sure Jeremy is safe. I have three more years before Jeremy is eighteen and goes to college, then I can think about dating."

"And what if someone else comes in and sweeps Nikolai off his feet in the meantime?" Sergei asked softly.

"I'm terrified that is going to happen, but there's nothing I can do about it right now. It's a risk I have to take. Jeremy comes first. I mean, how can I ask Nikolai out when my day is already full between work and taking care of my brother? He deserves better."

"Maybe you should let Nikolai make those decisions for himself instead of making him feel bad about himself, thinking you don't like him and find him distasteful."

Brandon scoffed. "Nikolai? His self-confidence is legendary. I'm sure he doesn't care what I think of him."

"Then you haven't been paying attention at all. Nikolai is very sensitive. He simply hides it behind snark and bravado."

Brandon paused to go over all his previous interactions with Nikolai before banging his head on the steering wheel again. "Damn it. I'll talk to him Saturday. I didn't mean to make him feel bad."

Sergei reached out and grabbed Brandon's shoulder, giving it a squeeze. "I know you didn't. Oh, and Brandon…" Sergei waited until Brandon looked over at him. "Bring your brother with you on Saturday. I want to meet him."

"Yes, sir."

* * * *

After a long afternoon of phone calls and meetings, Brandon was ready for some peace and quiet. He juggled the pizzas he'd picked up for dinner with his laptop bag as he tried to open the door from the garage into the house. He was met by the sound of a shoot-em-up video game being played at decibels that probably rivaled a true battle. It was good to see his brother was making full use of the surround sound. He set the pizzas on the breakfast bar and put his laptop bag on one of the three barstools before making his way to the doorway leading into the living room.

His brother was sprawled out on the couch with a game controller in his hand and a headset on. He was yelling into the attached microphone, telling someone named 'Bones' to 'watch his six'. Brandon could only shake his head at the noise and the mess surrounding his brother in a wide arc from where he sat. Soda bottles and decimated bags of snacks were scattered everywhere. He knew for a fact that the now-empty Dorito's bag had just been purchased the night before, along with the mostly empty package of Oreo's. He might have to ask Sergei for a raise at this rate. His grocery budget had certainly taken quite the hit over the last year as his brother grew — and grew.

A groan from his brother pulled his attention back to the screen where *Mission Failed* flashed. He took the opportunity to let his brother know he was there.

"Hey, Jeremy."

Jeremy jumped a foot in the air, comically putting his hand to his chest. "You scared the crap out of me."

"I scared the crap out of *you*? How is that possible? Do you even know how loud your game is?"

"I need the full experience, bro."

"The whole neighborhood doesn't need the full experience, *bro*, and you're cleaning up this mess after dinner."

Jeremy's expression brightened. "Yeah, okay. What's for dinner? I'm starving."

Brandon shot a disbelieving look at his brother then waved a hand at the carnage surrounding him. "How can you be starving?"

"I'm a growing boy. Feed me."

"Come to the kitchen. I picked up pizza."

"Yay! I've been wanting pizza. It's like you read my mind."

"Not that much of a leap. You always want pizza. You'd eat it every day if I let you."

"True." Jeremy charged into the kitchen in his usual exuberant way. He tripped over nothing but managed to right himself before he crashed into anything and threw himself onto one of the barstools at the breakfast bar. Brandon looked in the pizza boxes and handed Jeremy his before grabbing his own and sliding on to the stool next to him. They didn't stand on formality around there. *No sense dirtying a dish if we don't have to.*

"Hey, Jessie wants me to stay over Saturday night for a game night. Can I go?"

"Yeah. I don't see why not."

"Great. I'll tell him I can go with him after the soccer game Saturday morning then."

"Um, you can't do that. I'll drop you off in the afternoon. Sergei wants to meet you."

Jeremy paused with his slice of pizza halfway to his mouth. "You told Sergei about me?"

"Yep, and now he wants to meet you. I have a lunch meeting with him and Nikolai at Sergei's house. He said to bring you."

"Can't wait." Jeremy bounced in his seat a couple times before attacking his pizza again.

Brandon could only shake his head. Jeremy didn't seem to be fazed by anything. He lived his life constantly at full speed. The only time he wasn't moving was when he was sleeping—and even then he talked in his sleep most nights. The dream conversation his brother once had between a pirate and his parrot complete with separate voices for each of the characters was still his favorite. A person didn't exactly expect to hear "*Polly want a cracker*" in the middle of the night.

"The plan for Saturday will be the game, then home to shower and to Sergei's for lunch. If you have your bag packed, I can drop you off at Jessie's after lunch and the meeting. It is a kickoff discussion, so it shouldn't take long."

"Then maybe you can do something fun, bro. Maybe go out on a date or something."

"What?"

"You can do stuff on your own, you know. I'm not a baby anymore. You don't even have to hire a babysitter if you want to go out and do things."

"What the hell? You are the second person today who has told me I need to date. Where did this come from?"

"Dude. You don't think I know what you've given up to take care of me? You're twenty-eight. You should have been doing fun, single-guy things, not playing dad to your little brother."

"I wasn't playing at anything, Jer. It's been my privilege to take care of you."

"I know that, bro. I do. I couldn't ask for a better father figure, but I want you to be happy too."

"I *am* happy!"

"No. You're not *un*happy. There's a difference."

"Since when did you become this great, wise Yoda?"

Jeremy shrugged. "Katie at school was talking about how hard her parent's divorce has been on her mom. She said that her dad is already shacked up with someone else, but guys don't want to date her mom because she has a kid. It got me thinking about the fact that I've never seen you date. You stay home with me all the time. That's just wrong on so many levels."

Jeremy paused to shoot him a cheeky grin. "Besides, I need some space. You are totally harshing my mellow with all the 'Jeremy, take out the trash, Jeremy, clean up your mess'. Man, get a life. The world will keep spinning if we can't eat off the floor."

"All right, all right. That's enough. I'll think about it. Eat your pizza, so you can clean up your mess in the living room," Brandon finished with a smirk.

"Yeah. Yeah. On it, oh great slave driver."

Chapter Three

Nikolai stood in front of his locker at the dojo after his shower with a towel wrapped around his hips. He didn't usually shower there, preferring the privacy of his own home, but he didn't have a lot of time before he was due at Sergei's for lunch. Two of the three classes he taught on Saturday mornings had gone well. He loved teaching the little ones. His Little Tiger class for ages four to six was his absolute favorite, while at the same time driving him absolutely crazy. Their attention span was as short as they were.

The second class of the morning was a self-defense class for women. He hated that it was necessary, but he was glad to teach anyone who wanted to learn. He was chosen as the instructor of the class mainly because of his size. Master Jin had decided that his smaller stature would make the women feel more comfortable. Nikolai usually started the class having one of the other instructors come in too, however, so he could show that even though he was small, he could still defend himself. He hadn't earned his second-degree black belt by batting his eyes, no matter what people believed. He taught the same class on Thursday nights.

Most of the time his juniors' class of twelve to sixteen-year-olds that followed was a relief, as most of the students in the class were fairly serious about learning but were much more light-hearted about it. He frowned as he thought about how badly today's class had been, though. Two of the boys had gotten into an argument because apparently Shawn had decided to use the techniques he'd learned to torment a high school classmate, and fellow student Josh had found out and confronted him about it.

Nikolai ended up sending the boys to talk with Master Jin once he got them separated with the help of his teaching assistant. Nikolai didn't like having to put a submission hold on one of his own students, but it sounded like Shawn needed the lesson in humility anyway. Master Jin came in at the end of class to give the lecture about how the techniques taught were 'not to be used on those we perceive as weaker than us'. *Fun times...not.*

Nikolai tried to stretch the tight muscles in his neck by rolling his head in a circle. He had to go speak to Master Jin and find out what the results of the discussion were before he could leave, but he wasn't looking forward to it. With a deep sigh, Nikolai finished getting dressed in jeans and a plain T-shirt, putting his hair up in a messy bun. It wasn't his normal attire when he was heading out, but he didn't have the energy to put the effort into his normal look. What he had worn to the dojo that morning was good enough. He stuffed his gi and towel into his gym bag, making sure to put his belt in an outside pocket, before shouldering his bag and leaving the locker room.

Nikolai made his way to Master Jin's office, knocking on the door jamb when he got there. Master looked up from the papers on his desk and waved Nikolai in, pointing to the chair in front of him. Nikolai walked in and bowed before sitting.

"So, how bad was it, Master Jin?"

Master Jin winced. "Let's just say Shawn will no longer be in your juniors' class. He thought he had the right to pick on someone weaker than him, and when I pulled his father into the discussion, the man praised Shawn for putting the homo pipsqueak in his place. So, we know why the boy thinks the way he does." Nikolai quirked one eyebrow at his mentor. "Yeah, yeah, I know, Nikolai. You said six months ago he was going to be a problem, but I really thought I got through when I spoke to him then."

"What is it you always say, Master? *Saru mo ki kara ochiru.*"

"Yeah. Yeah. Even monkeys fall from trees. I just wish this particular monkey falling hadn't resulted in an innocent getting hurt."

Nikolai could only shake his head. "We do the best we can. I had hoped you'd gotten through to him too. You didn't this time, but you have gotten through to many."

"I guess so, but it still stings."

"I know. Well, I have to get going."

"What do you have going on today? You usually work out after your classes."

"Sergei wants me to work with his assistant Brandon on a special project to open an LGBTQ center here in Raleigh." Nikolai winced. "He wanted me to ask if you or one of the instructors here would be interested in teaching self-defense classes once we opened."

"What? Doesn't he know you're a second-degree black belt?"

"Nope. I'm not sure what my family thinks I've been doing here all these years, but actually working at it isn't one of them."

"Well, now might be a good time to let them know, Nik."

"I'll think about it. I like having something that's just mine. No one here knows my last name. I'm not a Barinov here. I'm Nik, and I don't have to be anything but Nik."

"While I appreciate that the dojo is your safe place, I think you need to start bringing all the pieces of yourself together. You're starting to fray a little bit."

"What do you mean?"

"You're heading to Sergei's for lunch?"

"Yeah. So?"

"You realize you have no makeup on, right?"

"I know, but as I said, Brandon is going to be there and he's not comfortable with the swishy me."

"Which is my point. You need to stop splitting your personality and only letting certain people see certain sides of you. It's not your job to make everyone comfortable."

"I know. I'm working on it."

"That's all I ask," Master Jin said seriously before his gaze lit with amusement. "Get out of here and try not to embarrass yourself in front of Brandon."

"Gah. Now that I make no promises about. I am such a dork whenever he is around. It's so embarrassing."

"Well, maybe working with him will get you over being awestruck, and you can start a friendship, if nothing else."

"Friendship? I want to have his babies."

Master Jin laughed outright at that. "You do realize you don't have the right plumbing for that, right?"

"Whatever." Nikolai stood and gave Master Jin another bow. "Hope the rest of the afternoon goes better for both of us."

"Good luck. Call me if you need to talk."

"Thanks."

Nikolai re-shouldered his bag and made his way out to his car. Climbing in, he started the engine and plugged in his phone. Using voice commands, he instructed the phone to call Sergei.

"Hey, Nikolai. Are you on your way?"

"Yep. Just checking to see if you needed me to pick up anything."

"Nope. We're all set. Brandon called a few minutes ago and said he and Jeremy are ten minutes out."

"Who's Jeremy?" *Please don't say Brandon is bringing a boyfriend with him.*

"Jeremy is Brandon's brother. It seems Brandon's been keeping secrets. He's been raising his little brother."

"Really? How old is he?"

"Fifteen, from what Brandon said."

Nikolai couldn't hold back his chuckle as a feeling of relief swept through him. "Are you sure you have enough food then? Fifteen is bottomless-pit age."

"Yes," Sergei snarked back. "I'm sure I have enough food for everyone. Just get here."

"On my way, Bossman."

Sergei hung-up without replying.

"Well, this should be interesting. Who knew?"

Chapter Four

Brandon followed his brother up the sidewalk to Sergei's door. Jeremy hadn't stopped talking since his soccer game. Scoring the winning goal had led to a very chatty little brother and required a play-by-play analysis of the whole match.

"You do remember I was there and watched the entire thing, right?"

"I know. I know. I'm just so excited. Did you see how sweet that last play was? It was just like we practiced it."

"Well, that's a good thing. It's nice when things work the way they're planned."

"Yep. Yep." Jeremy stood bouncing on his toes in front of the door. "What do you think he made for lunch?"

"No idea, but you will be appreciative of whatever it is. Got it?" Brandon gave him a stern look to accompany the words, hoping to impress his seriousness on his brother.

Jeremy rolled his eyes at him. "I'm not two. I know what to do."

Brandon gave him another stern look as he pressed the doorbell. "Best behavior. I mean it, Jeremy."

"I got this, bro. Chill."

A snort of amusement had Brandon turning to look behind him. He hadn't heard Nikolai's arrival. Brandon narrowed his eyes at Nikolai, trying to figure out what was different. "Where's your makeup?"

Nikolai shrugged. "It makes you uncomfortable, so I decided to leave it off today. No big deal."

Brandon scowled back at Nikolai, but the door opened, and Sergei's booming voice interrupted before he could respond.

"Great. You all made it. You must be Jeremy. Sergei Barinov. I am so pleased to meet you."

Jeremy took Sergei's offered hand and shook it very solemnly. "Nice to meet you, Mr. Barinov. I've heard a lot about you. My brother loves working for you."

"Well, while I can't say I've heard a lot about you, we are going to start changing that right now. Please, call me Sergei. I have a feeling we are going to be great friends. Now come in, everyone. Lunch is almost ready."

"What's for lunch?" Nikolai asked Sergei as he was walking down the hall to the kitchen.

"Stuart made lasagna — and a lot of it. I was warned fifteen-year-olds require a lot of food."

Jeremy snickered as he followed everyone. "I'm guessing my brother was the one who warned you of that."

"Your brother, my mother, Nikolai, Stuart. Just pick a name of anyone in my life and they probably said something to that effect."

"That's amazing." Brandon was happy to see that Jeremy still had a huge smile on his face when he walked into the kitchen.

Stuart was busy taking a large pan of lasagna out of the oven and setting it on top of the stove next to another large pan of the same. He picked up a tray of garlic bread from the counter and placed it in the oven and set the timer before turning to greet everyone.

"Hey, guys. Just need a few minutes on the garlic bread, and we will be ready to go. You must be Jeremy." Stuart extended his hand to shake. "I'm Stuart, Sergei's better half."

"It's great to finally meet you," Jeremy replied. "Brandon says you have an awesome gaming system and that you love to go to comic-cons. Brandon got me tickets for Animazement here in Raleigh over Memorial Day weekend this year. Do you go?"

"Yep. I go every year. I'm still trying to decide what I want to dress up as. Maybe we can discuss it while these three are doing boring work stuff."

Jeremy bounced on his toes with excitement. "That sounds great."

Brandon shared an amused look with Sergei before turning back to Stuart. "Now that that's settled, it's nice to see you again, Stuart."

"Great to see you, too. I've been so busy that I haven't been able to go by the office lately.

"It's all good. We've been swamped as well, so I probably wouldn't have been able to chat much anyway. Your man keeps me hopping."

"Ha," Jeremy interjected. "You wouldn't know what to do with yourself if you weren't hopping. You don't know how to chill."

"That's true. I can't deny it, but it keeps you in Dorito's."

"And I greatly appreciate that." Jeremy nodded enthusiastically. "Keep him busy, Sergei."

Brandon couldn't help but laugh at Jeremy's sincerity. Shaking his head, he pointed a finger at his brother. "See what I have to put up with?"

"I, for one, think it's great. I'm so glad to meet him," Stuart said.

"Now all we have to do is get my brother to find a guy to start dating and life will be good."

Brandon felt himself blushing as he heard Nikolai squeak, "A guy?"

All humor dropped from Jeremy's expression as he glared at Nikolai. "Yeah, Brandon is gay. Do you have a problem with it?"

Brandon was quick to jump in. "Easy, Jeremy. Everyone here is gay or bi."

"Oh. Sorry." Jeremy looked contrite as he addressed Nikolai.

"It's okay. I've just never seen Brandon date a guy."

"Brandon hasn't dated *anyone*. The only people he even meets for lunch or dinner are some of his friends from college. He really needs to get a life outside of work and me."

"Hmm, where have you heard that before?" Sergei smirked at Brandon as he said it.

"Yeah. Yeah," Brandon intoned dryly. "I'm ruining my brother's life by not giving him time by himself and forcing him to do his chores. I'm a horrible, horrible person."

"That's not the point, and you know it." Sergei clapped his hand on Brandon's shoulder as the timer went off, and Stuart turned to remove the garlic bread from the oven. "We just want you happy."

"Come on, everyone. Let's give poor Brandon a break. Lunch is ready." Brandon shot Stuart a thankful look, which he met with a raised eyebrow and a headshake.

Nikolai was strangely quiet during lunch, keeping his head down and focusing on eating. Brandon noticed that he wasn't the only one shooting the man concerned glances. Finally, when he couldn't stand it anymore, he set down his fork and knife and turned so he was facing him directly. "What's up with you?"

Nikolai startled and met his gaze. "I don't know what you mean?"

"First, no makeup, and you're dressed...I don't know, not like you. There is no pizazz to that outfit at all."

"Pizazz?" Nikolai chuckled. "Who uses the word 'pizazz'?"

"I do." Brandon crossed his arms defensively. "Don't deflect."

"I've just had a rough morning is all."

"You also said you didn't wear makeup because it makes me uncomfortable."

"You can't deny it does."

"Yes, but not because I don't like it."

"What?"

"What do you mean 'what'? You have to know you're gorgeous."

"I am?"

Brandon was blown away by the absolute surprise on Nikolai's face, before he scowled. "Stop fishing for compliments. You know you are."

"It's nice to know you think so. Thank you."

Brandon couldn't tear his gaze away from Nikolai's shy smile and the obvious pleasure at his comments — that was until Sergei's voice made them both jump and turn to look at him.

"What do you mean you had a rough morning?" Sergei asked.

Stuart smacked him on the shoulder. "Can't you see they were having a moment?"

"I wanted to know why he had a rough morning. It's concern."

Brandon couldn't hold back his chuckle at Sergei's indignant tone. "It's all good. I want to know the answer to that, too."

He turned back to look at Nikolai to find Nikolai biting his lip and obviously debating with himself about something, before rolling his eyes and making some sort of decision. He whispered what sounded like "All right, Sensei, all right," which made no sense before squaring his shoulders and facing Sergei.

"Two of my students at the dojo got into a fight today. One of them had been using what he was learning to harass a classmate at school. The other student took offense — as he should have."

"What do you mean one of your students?" Sergei cut in, sounding absolutely shocked.

"I teach two self-defense classes for women, one Tiny Tiger class and one Junior Tiger class at the dojo. I also take class there two days a week."

"That's what you do there?"

"I go four days a week, Sergei. What did you think I did there?" Nikolai looked equal parts amused and insulted as he asked the question.

Stuart spoke before Sergei could reply. "You said he's been going since he was twelve, Sergei, and you know what a perfectionist he is. Did you really think he wasn't at least a black belt by now? What level are you, anyway?"

Nikolai dropped his gaze back to his plate as a blush came up on his cheeks. "Um. Second-degree black belt. I test for my third-degree sometime this year."

"What?" Sergei's bellow shocked them all.

"What do you mean 'what'? I think it's pretty self-explanatory."

Sergei counted off on his fingers. "First, you didn't let me know when you defended your thesis. Second, I find out you are a second-degree black belt, and you have never mentioned it? What the hell, Nikolai?"

What followed next was a slew of Russian back and forth between Nikolai and Sergei that left Brandon looking on in bewilderment. Jeremy obviously shared his confusion from the quick peek he took at his expression, while Stuart looked on in amusement. Finally, Stuart put two fingers to his lips and a sharp whistle rang out. Sergei stopped with his mouth wide open and turned an irritated glance on his fiancé. Stuart smirked at Sergei and shook his head.

"You are both being quite rude. We have guests, and you are talking in a language that you know we don't understand. If you are going to argue, it at least must be in English so we can follow along."

Nikolai and Sergei each took a deep breath and exhaled loudly, making Jeremy giggle. Brandon pressed his lips together to keep from laughing himself. He didn't think this was an appropriate time.

"You know you're not funny, *kotik*. Not funny at all, but I apologize to all of you anyway, because he is right."

"I apologize as well," Nikolai added, still with a hint of an accent, which unlike Sergei, he didn't usually have. "It was quite rude of us to argue in front of you in the first place, let alone in another language."

Brandon surprised himself by reaching out and laying his hand on Nikolai's arm. The jolt of connection caused him to flinch. He could have kicked himself when he saw the look of quickly masked hurt in Nikolai's eyes. He tentatively extended his hand again palm up and waited for Nikolai to warily place his in it before speaking. "I want to know why you hide all these pieces of yourself. Didn't you think Sergei would be supportive — or your friends, for that matter?"

"You're freaking me out a little here. Why are you being so nice to me?"

"Well, it bothers me that you would hide pieces of yourself from not only me, but from everyone else. Plus, do you want full disclosure?"

Nikolai nodded. "Of course. Honesty is important."

Brandon raised an eyebrow at Nikolai, earning an eye roll.

"Yeah. Yeah. Do as I say, not as I do. Just tell me already," Nikolai insisted.

"Sergei pointed out that my plan to wait to date until my brother was in college has some major flaws. Mainly, that someone else could come in and swoop you up if I wait. I can't let that happen."

"Really? You want to date *me*?"

"I do. I had it in my head that I needed to focus on work and my brother. I wanted to be able to give you the attention you deserve, but that's stupid. All relationships have give and take. My brother is an important part of my life, and you wouldn't be the man I think you are if you had a problem with it."

"Of course, I wouldn't have a problem with it. He's part of what makes you...well, you. You're a caretaker. You do an amazing job with Sergei and obviously with your brother as well, since he adores you."

Brandon shot a look at Jeremy to see he was watching the exchange with fascination. "Well, most of the time."

"Yeah, except when he makes me do chores and homework."

"It's my job, Jeremy."

"Yeah. Yeah. Don't talk to me. Continue with the sweet talking." Jeremy then stage whispered, "I think it's working."

Nikolai stage-whispered back, "I think you're right." Then in his normal voice, "How about we all finish lunch? Your brother and I can discuss this more later."

"I'm spending the night at my friend's house tonight. Just saying."

Everyone burst into laughter, and Brandon relaxed his shoulders. He had to admit he'd been a little worried about what Jeremy would think of Nikolai. There was knowing your brother was gay then seeing your brother with a guy. Obviously, he had worried for nothing. Jeremy seemed to have taken it all in stride. Brandon had to reluctantly let go of Nikolai's hand so he could pick up his fork. Looking at Nikolai, he got a wink, before Nikolai also picked up his.

"So, the dude who got in trouble for using his techniques against classmates... Was that Shawn Masterson?"

"How did you...?"

"I go to school with him...and Josh. Shawn was picking on my best friend Jessie at school Friday and got him in some kind of hold, showing off to his friends until Josh showed up. He said something about talking to Master Nik at class. Shawn told him to go ahead, what did he care?"

"Well, he won't be attending class at my dojo anymore."

"You kicked him out?"

"Master Jin did. We don't condone that behavior. It's meant for exercise, defense and mind-focusing, not bullying."

"Cool. I can't wait to tell Jessie." Jeremy bounced in his seat a few times, before turning to Stuart. "Can I have some more lasagna? It's really good."

"And that, gentlemen, is the attention span of a teenager." Brandon waved in Jeremy's direction. "They can only focus on a subject so long before they must be fed."

Stuart laughed as he stood up, grabbed Jeremy's plate and made his way to the stove where he scooped up another serving of the savory food.

"Hey, I'm a growing boy."

"I'm well aware. My food budget has quadrupled in the last six months." He shook his head as Jeremy snickered before attacking a piece of garlic bread like he hadn't eaten in a month. "All kidding aside," Brandon continued as Stuart walked back to the table, "everything is really good. I'm impressed."

"Thanks. It's one of the dishes I can make well."

"Don't sell yourself short, *kotik*. You are an excellent cook."

"What does *kotik* mean?"

Sergei smirked at Jeremy. "It means 'kitten'."

Jeremy choked on the bite of lasagna he had just taken, reaching out and grabbing his drink once he got his choking under control. "Really? He doesn't look like a kitten at all. I thought you were going to say 'lion' or 'tiger' or something."

"Yeah, well, my fiancé has a very warped sense of humor. Just realize it's a thing in this family and move on. It's the only way to survive," Stuart explained.

"Yep. Sad, but true," Nikolai added while nodding his head. "Except me, of course. I have a well-defined comedy palate."

Sergei pointed his fork at Nikolai. "Really? Wasn't it you who gave everyone whoopie cushions for Christmas one year?"

"I was eight. That is the height of comedy at eight. You can't hold that against me!"

"Okay. I guess I can cut you a little slack on that one."

"I think that's funny now," Jeremy responded. "Why didn't you ever get me whoopie cushions, Bran?"

"Because knowing you, you would take them to school and put them on your teachers' and friends' chairs."

"And the principal's. That would be epic."

"That would *not* be epic. That would be detention."

Jeremy thought for a moment before nodding decisively. "I think it would be worth it."

"Would it be worth it to lose your gaming privileges for a month?"

Jeremy sagged in his seat, looking completely dejected. "No."

Brandon hid his smirk behind a napkin and noticed the others were all working very hard not to make eye contact with each other. Stuart was staring at his drink, and Sergei was cutting his piece of lasagna with great precision, while Nikolai had picked up the saltshaker and was staring at the white plastic dispenser like it held the secrets of the universe.

The buzzing of a cell phone had everyone pulling out their phones to see whose it was. It turned out Jeremy was the winner. "Hey, Mrs. P. What's up?" Pause. "What? Is he going to be okay?" Pause. "Did you call the police?" Pause. "Okay. Well, please let me know what happens. I'll talk to Jessie tomorrow. Thanks for calling, Mrs. P."

Brandon was concerned with how pale his brother had gotten. "What's going on?"

"That was Jessie's mom. She said Shawn Masterson went over to their house, confronted Jessie and beat him up because he said it was Jessie's fault that he was kicked out of the dojo. The police arrested Shawn, and Jessie is at the hospital with a broken nose, probably a broken arm and a possible concussion from where Shawn kicked him." Jeremy turned emotion-filled eyes toward Brandon. "Why would he do that?"

Nikolai answered before Brandon could come up with a response. "Sometimes people just suck. The reason I started karate was because of a guy like Shawn — someone who thought that because they were bigger and stronger, it gave them the right to bully me."

"Who? Who did that?" Sergei's expression as he asked the question promised some serious consequences.

Nikolai waved his hand in the air. "It doesn't matter now. I avoided him until I had the skills to put him in his place. I honestly think a lot of this is coming from Shawn's dad, though. His father is" — a pause and deep sigh from Nikolai — "not a nice man. I have seen Shawn be really decent from time to time — helping some of the younger kids figure out a move, helping clean up without anyone asking, things like that. It usually happens when he is staying with his mom, since his parents have joint custody and he switches back and forth, but still...he does have it in him. That doesn't give him a pass on the bad things he's done, but I understand getting pressure from a parent."

"What do you mean?" Jeremy asked.

"My father is not very gay friendly. He pretends to be when Sergei is around, but he's really not. I came out when I was sixteen, and he didn't really believe me. He said I was only doing it because Sergei said he was bi. He tried to convince me I wasn't gay and talked about sending me to one of those gay conversion camps. It was not a good time."

Jeremy's, "What happened?" was drowned out by Sergei's, "What the hell?"

"Don't worry, Sergei. Your mom stepped in. She came to the house and told my father he was being an asshole and had me pack up my things and come stay with them for a while. We told everyone I was there to help entertain the littles for the summer, but it was really to get me away from my parents."

"That's why you were there?"

Nikolai shrugged. "Yep. Best summer of my life, honestly. Your mom is great."

"Yes, she is," Stuart replied.

"But you had to go back home at the end of the summer?"

"Yeah, but Sergei's mom made sure my parents knew that they were to treat me with respect or she would go to Sergei."

"Then what happened?" Jeremy was sitting forward in his seat and listening attentively.

"My parents told me that they would allow me to live at home, as long as I didn't talk about being gay."

"What did you do?"

To Brandon's surprise, Nikolai started chuckling. "I didn't talk about being gay, but I decided to make myself into the gayest gay boy who ever gayed. I started wearing makeup and dressing in over-the-top extra everything. Usually I have makeup and am stylish with a side of sassy clothes on. I save T-shirts and no make-up for when I'm at home or at the dojo."

"Do you like to wear the makeup and stuff?"

"Yes, actually. It makes me feel good, but I like to keep it simple too. Sometimes it seems like too much work, but I have a reputation to uphold," Nikolai finished with a wink and a smirk.

"Well, you do you, dude. Whatever makes you happy," Jeremy offered.

"Thank you, Jeremy. I appreciate you saying that."

"I tell Jessie that all the time..." Jeremy looked stricken for a moment, like he hadn't meant to say anything.

Brandon reached out and set his hand on Jeremy's shoulder. "Jeremy, is Jessie gay?"

"Yeah, but please don't say anything. He hasn't told his mom yet."

"I wouldn't say anything. It's his decision when he tells people. What about you?"

"What about me?" Jeremy looked genuinely confused by the question.

"Are you gay?"

"Oh no. I like girls, but him being gay doesn't have anything to do with me—like you being gay." Jeremy shrugged. "Jessie's my best friend. End of story."

"Out of the mouths of babes," Stuart whispered.

"Brandon, how long do you think Jessie will be at the hospital?"

"It will depend on how busy it is there today."

"Oh." Jeremy slumped in his seat.

"Why don't you text Jessie's mom and see if we can maybe bring them something over for dinner? How would that be?"

"That would be great. Thanks, Brandon."

Chapter Five

Jeremy pulled out his phone and started texting furiously as Nikolai watched. He hadn't quite meant to bare his soul to everyone, but Sensei's words had rung true somewhere down deep. He couldn't keep all his different pieces separate anymore. It was exhausting — so many secrets, so many different aspects of his personality.

Brandon had been a complete surprise. He honestly hadn't thought Brandon liked him. For that matter, he had thought Brandon was straight until two hours before. His gaydar always had been non-existent though, so it wasn't really a surprise if he thought about it. Nikolai had gotten to the point that he didn't even try to hit on anyone. His college friends always made fun of him because he always managed to pick the one straight guy to hit on wherever they went. It was a skillset for sure. *Cue eyeroll.*

Nikolai allowed himself to look at Brandon while he was interacting with his brother. That had been another surprise. It showed that he had actually picked a good guy to have a crush on all these years. *Man, has it been years?* Nikolai counted back in his head. *Shit. It's been four years. Oh well, I might as well accept it. I'm not getting over it any time soon.*

Brandon glanced up and saw Nikolai staring at him. "What?"

"You're a really good dad slash big brother." Nikolai was fascinated by the blush he could barely see on Brandon's cheeks.

"It's hard work, but we've been figuring it out as we go along."

"He's right, you know," Stuart interjected. "You're doing a great job with him. That is one well-grounded kid."

Jeremy put down his phone before they could all embarrass Brandon any further.

"Jessie's mom says they are still at the hospital. The good news is that there's no concussion. The bad news is that his arm and nose are definitely broken. They have reset the nose and are waiting for the orthopedic doc to look at the X-rays to determine if they are going to cast or splint the arm. She says no on the food tonight, since she doesn't know when they will get out of there, but maybe I could come over after the game tomorrow and keep Jessie company."

"Game?" Sergei asked.

"Yeah. I have another soccer game tomorrow at one-thirty. Jessie was supposed to be there, too."

"Well, tell his mom that you'll text after the game and make sure it's still okay."

"Okay." Jeremy bent his head and texted for a few moments longer, before looking back up at his brother. "Guess you won't have the house to yourself tonight after all. Sorry."

"Eh. There will be other nights, Jer."

Stuart clapped his hands together. "Okay. Well, let's clean up then you all can talk about your big project. Jeremy and I have Animazement plans to discuss. After everyone is done, maybe we can have a game night or something. How does that sound?"

"Anything but Monopoly," Nikolai and Jeremy said together.

"Why don't you like Monopoly, Jeremy?" Stuart asked.

Jeremy winced. "Brandon is horribly cutthroat at Monopoly. It's not fun."

"Yeah. Sergei is the same," Nikolai added with a wince. "Playing with him is brutal. There was this one time when I was like seven and I had gotten the game for my birthday. Sergei wiped me out. It wasn't a good time."

"And no one will play with me since then," Sergei interjected dejectedly.

"Sergei, that fake pout is not attractive," Nikolai said.

Sergei looked at Stuart and his fiancé winced. "Yeah, babe. That is not a good look for you."

"I'll play Monopoly with you one day, Bossman. These guys don't know what they're missing."

"Um, yeah, we do. A horrible boring time with my brother and his boss."

Nikolai offered Jeremy a fist bump. "Preach." After Jeremy tapped his fist, Nikolai waved at his plate. "Are you done eating?"

"Yeah. I'm good."

"Then let's clean up."

Everyone stood and cleared the space, with Stuart packing the leftovers into containers.

"Nikolai, the purple container is full of leftovers for you. Brandon, the bigger green container is for you and Jeremy to take with you when you leave."

"What about you?" Jeremy asked.

"I have another whole lasagna in the freezer for Sergei and me. It's easy enough to make multiple pans when you are making one already."

"Cool. Thanks, Stuart. I really liked it."

"Maybe I can teach you how to make it some time, Jeremy."

"That would be awesome. I like to cook, but Brandon and I don't know what we're doing too much. We stick to basics, for the most part."

"Well, we will have to get Sergei and-or Saul's mom to teach you some things too. They are both way better than me."

Jeremy bounced on his toes for a moment. "Who's Saul?"

"Saul Valencia is married to my best friend Lee. He used to be a professional football player. Lee works at the garage with Nikolai."

"Oh, yeah. I remember Brandon talking about him now, about how he had to come out because someone was trying to blackmail him about being gay. That sucked. If you think they would teach me, that would be great."

"They will be happy to have someone else to teach. Prepare to be adopted. Now, you three go on into the living room. Jeremy and I have important things to discuss." Stuart pecked Sergei on the cheek before grabbing him by the shoulder and turning him around, ending with a slap to his ass. "Get moving, Barinov."

"Do you see how he treats me? Always trying to get rid of me."

Nikolai couldn't help the snort of laughter that escaped. "Riiiiight. Like you two aren't usually joined at the hip."

Brandon turned a snicker into a cough. "It's like they're drawn together like magnets, isn't it?"

Nikolai snapped his fingers. "That's it exactly."

"You two are not funny...not funny at all." Sergei's scowl was fierce, but Nikolai knew that Sergei was all bark and no bite, and obviously Brandon knew it too, if the grin on his face was any indication.

Sergei's growled, "Let's get to work," caused Nikolai to grin even wider, making his cheeks hurt.

Nikolai gave Sergei a jaunty salute as he passed by him into the living room. "Sir! Yes, sir!"

"Smartass. Why do I put up with you again?"

"Um-m. Because I'm cute?"

"Nope, that's not it. You're not that cute."

"Fake gasp. I'm hurt. It's probably because I make you money then."

"Yep. That's the only reason I tolerate you." Sergei reached out and attempted to put Nikolai in a headlock, but Nikolai evaded him and did a move that bent his hand back and brought Sergei to his knees instead. Sergei's squawk of outrage was music to Nikolai's ears.

"Admit you love me, and I'll let you go."

"Never. I don't care what ninja moves you do to me. I will never surrender."

Nikolai shifted his grip and placed Sergei in a slightly more awkward and painful hold, earning a yelp from Sergei. "Admit you love me!"

"All right. All right. I love you. Why? I don't know. Now let me go."

Nikolai leaned down and gave Sergei a smacking kiss on the top of his head, before releasing him and stepping back. "I love you, too, you big Russian cuddle bear."

Jeremy was jumping up and down in his excitement. "That was amazing! You're so much smaller than him, but you took him down. He couldn't even *move*. Could you teach Jessie how to do that, so he doesn't get hurt again?"

"Sure. Have Brandon find out a time that works for him to meet me at the dojo. I can teach him a few things. Then if he wants to continue, we can get him into one of the classes."

"That would be great. I can't wait to tell him."

Sergei grabbed the bottom of his shirt and tugged to straighten it as he stood back up. "Yes. Wonderful. Glad I could show you the benefits of self-defense classes. Now we must get to work or we will be here all night."

Nikolai snickered under his breath. "Yep. It was all part of Sergei's master plan."

Sergei gave Nikolai a look that promised retribution, as Stuart walked up and gave Sergei a quick hug. "On that note... Come on, Jeremy. Let's head to my office. I don't think we need to see anymore."

Jeremy chattered excitedly to Stuart as they walked down the hallway to Stuart's office. Having been in there before, Nikolai knew Jeremy was going to love all the gaming and convention items Stuart had on display. He knew he was right when Jeremy yelled, "O...M...G!"

The pause Jeremy put between the letters indicating his awe at what he was seeing had the three remaining adults all laughing. Once they had themselves under control, Sergei pointed to the couch. "Come on. Let's get comfortable. I have folders of information for you to go through."

Nikolai headed to his favorite recliner in the room. It was designed for a much bigger person, but Nikolai loved how he could snuggle into it. Brandon sat on the end of the couch closest to him, while Sergei grabbed the folders and handed them out. After pushing the button to raise the footrest on the recliner, Nikolai made himself comfortable and started to read.

"This is really good information, Sergei. You've obviously been thinking about this for a while."

"Thank you, Nik. It's a pet project of mine, for sure. It was a niggle about something I needed to do, but then when I heard Stuart had been kicked out of his house at eighteen and was lucky that his uncle took him in, it brought home for me how important a center like this is for this city. It just made it more imperative for me to do."

"It would have been nice to have had someplace I could have gone when I was young too. Even though I wasn't kicked out, home wasn't a pleasant place to be."

Nikolai turned to look at Brandon more closely. "I figured, since you have custody of your brother, but what happened to your parents?"

"Well...my mother is still alive, as far as I know. She has an addiction problem that started after my father died when I was eight. He was a police officer for the city and was shot and killed during a motor vehicle stop. Her doctor prescribed her something to help her sleep, then she needed pills to help her wake up and it went downhill from there. She actually managed to stay clean while she was pregnant with Jeremy. It was a good time for me and reminded me of the mom she used to be, but she went right back to the alcohol and drugs shortly after Jeremy was born. She said she couldn't handle the crying. I have no idea who Jeremy's father is. I don't think she knows either. She has always said she doesn't, at any rate."

"Jeremy is very lucky to have you. It can't have been easy suing your mom for custody."

"It wasn't pleasant. She said some really horrible things to me both before and during court." Brandon shrugged. "The end result was I got custody of Jeremy, though, and have been able to give him a stable homelife." Brandon got a faraway look in his eyes for a moment before visibly shaking himself and focusing back on Nikolai. "I don't want Jeremy to ever worry about where he is going to sleep or where his next meal will come from."

"No kid should have to worry about those things," Nikolai said softly.

"No, they really shouldn't. That's why I think Sergei's project here is so important."

Sergei's voice startled Nikolai. He had forgotten he was there. "I'm sorry for everything you've been through, but I'm happy it led to you working for me. I don't think I could do all this without you."

"Me too. You're a great boss," Brandon responded earnestly.

"Aw, that's so sweet, you two," Nikolai cooed. "Sergei, give him a hug."

Sergei crossed his arms over his chest. "I am not giving Brandon a hug."

"Nikolai! He's blushing. You made him blush."

Nikolai raised his hand to his mouth and blew on his nails before rubbing them on his shirtfront. "It's a skill."

"If you two are done...?" Sergei gave them both stern looks, before continuing. "Do you have any questions about the information in the folders?"

Brandon cleared his throat before answering Sergei. "No, sir."

"No sir, Mr. Grumpapotomus."

Sergei shook his head while pinching the bridge of his nose between the index finger and thumb of his right hand. "I need the two of you to take point on this."

"Why aren't you going to work on it, since it's your pet project?"

"I am unfortunately tied up with the takeover of Trinity Corporation."

"I'm confused. Why are you taking them over?" Nikolai asked. "I don't remember them on the list of potentials."

Nikolai saw Brandon turn his back on Sergei and subtly shake his head while mouthing 'no', then doing a facepalm when Sergei puffed up and started answering the question.

"Well, I'm glad you asked." Sergei then went on a rant of epic proportions about how the CEO of the company was a waste of space and resources and had provided funding to an anti-LGBTQ hate group, which was picketing one of Sergei's construction sites.

"Okay. Okay. I've got it. The owner is an anti-gay douche-monkey. You take him down and Brandon and I will work on the center. Really hit him where it hurts."

"Which was my plan," Sergei huffed. "I will leave the center to the two of you. As you saw, there are two potential sites for it. Take a look at both locations and get back to me with your thoughts. I'm going to go check on Stuart and Jeremy. I think I heard them go upstairs, probably to look at costumes. You two get started. Let me know any questions."

Nikolai waited until Sergei left the room before turning to Brandon. "Wow. Sorry. That's thirty minutes of my life I will never get back."

"Yeah. The CEO of the other company *is* a piece of work, but Sergei overheard him insulting both Stuart and his mother at the last Chamber of Commerce meeting. He didn't know Sergei was there."

"Ouch." Nikolai winced. "That's not good. Sergei is going to destroy him."

"Yep. Oh, and Sergei said something about having you attend the next meeting with him."

"Let me guess. In my finest attire, perhaps?"

"Oh yeah."

"I'll put it on the calendar."

Nik's phone started buzzing in his pocket. When he pulled it out, he was surprised to see Sensei's number on the screen. He could count on one hand the number of times Sensei had called him. Sensei believed in short and to the point text messages that usually amounted to 'come see me' and face-to-face conversations.

"Sensei. What's up?"

"I need you to come down to the dojo. The police are here asking about what happened here today with Shawn. It seems he — "

"I know, Sensei. I heard already. Brandon's brother is best friends with the kid he hurt. I'll be right there."

Hanging up, Nik stood and looked down at Brandon. "I'm afraid I won't be able to stay. That was Sensei. The police are there wanting to take a statement about today. Can you tell everyone I had to go? Sensei sounds the most stressed I've ever heard him."

Brandon stood up as well. "Sure. I'm sorry you have to leave. Game night would have been fun, but let's plan to meet up soon."

"Just for the center?"

"Um. No. If you agree, I'd like to take you out on a date."

Nik wiped his sweaty palms on his pant legs and took a step closer to Brandon. "Yeah? I mean...I'd like that."

Brandon also took a step closer and cleared his throat. "Yeah?"

"Definitely." The two of them had crept close enough to each other at this point, that Nikolai could touch Brandon if he wanted to — and man, did he want to. *Is Brandon leaning in? Is he?*

The two of them jumped apart when Jeremy came barreling down the stairs. "Brandon! You have got to see all the costumes Stuart has. He says I can borrow one for Animazement if I want. Look!"

Brandon shot Nikolai an apologetic look. "Be right there."

"You coming, Nik?"

"No, Jeremy. I have to go. The police want me to make a statement about Shawn."

"Oh, man. That stinks. You coming back?"

"Sadly, probably not. I have no idea how long this is going to take."

Jeremy paused for a moment. "You want to come to my game tomorrow? It would be nice to have more than just Brandon there to cheer me on."

Nikolai shot a look at Brandon. "If it's okay with your brother, I would love to."

"It would be great if you could," Brandon was quick to answer. "I can bring you an extra folding chair if you need one."

Nikolai chuckled. "The number of games I have attended for Sergei's younger brother, I have invested in my own gear. Comfort is key."

"Oh. I hear ya. I forgot that Sasha plays too."

"Yep."

"Great. Well, the game is at one o'clock. I'll send you the field information when I get home. I don't remember which one it is at off the top of my head."

"Can't wait. I'll meet you guys there." Nikolai jerked a thumb in the direction of the door. "I should head out. They're waiting for me at the dojo. I'll see you tomorrow. Tell Sergei bye for me and thank Stuart again for a delicious lunch, okay?"

"Yep. I got it."

Nikolai couldn't resist one more glance over his shoulder at Brandon as he went to open the door. He jolted when he realized Brandon was standing there watching him go. He turned his head forward in time to jump back before he hit himself in the face with the door. He shot a sheepish look at Brandon before shaking his head at himself and closing the door behind him.

Chapter Six

Jessie and his mother crossed the soccer field to where Brandon was set up to watch Jeremy play. Jessie's mother was carrying two folding chairs, so obviously they were there to root on the team as well. Jessie had a purple cast on the lower half of his left arm that matched the purple highlights in his hair and was sporting some pretty amazing black eyes.

"Dude, the black eyes and nose brace really make your green eyes pop."

"Jeremy!" Brandon was appalled his brother would say such a thing, but Jessie and his mother simply laughed.

Jessie raised his right hand toward his face as he winced. "Ow. Don't make me laugh, dude! That hurts."

Jeremy was immediately contrite. "How are you feeling?"

"Sore, but not too bad, really. Going to be at school tomorrow, at any rate."

"Here, Mrs. P. Let me get those for you." Jeremy proceeded to grab the chairs and set them up next to Brandon. "How long until you can play again?"

"I'm going to miss the rest of the season. Can't afford to get the nose hit again. Too much of a risk, even with the face shield."

"Yeah. I can see that. Too bad. You can be our cheerleader, at any rate."

"Yeah, I can do that."

Brandon turned his attention to Jessie's mother as the boys went off on a discussion of the other team. "Hi, Meghan. How are you doing through all this?"

"Better now that I know he's going to be okay. It was scary."

"I'm sure. I don't even know what I would do if something like that were to happen to Jeremy." Brandon snapped his fingers. "By the way, did Jeremy say anything to Jessie about the offer for self-defense lessons from Nik? He's the instructor at the dojo Shawn has been banned from."

Meghan tightened her mouth in anger. "He told me, but why should I let my son step one foot in a place that taught that monster to hurt people?"

"Whoa. Whoa. Whoa. It's not like that at all. Nik says what they teach isn't for bullying or hurting other people. It's only supposed to be for focus and self-defense. He had been warned once before, and they kicked Shawn out as soon as they found out what he had done at the school."

"Yeah, Mrs. P, Nik is really cool. He's gay and has dealt with bullies and stuff. That's why he started training."

"He's gay?" Meghan shot a look at Jessie. Brandon had a moment to wonder what that look meant before Jeremy kept speaking.

"Yeah. He's going to be dating my brother. I like him."

"You're gay, Brandon?" Meghan looked shocked at this piece of information.

"Yes. I've made no secret of it." Brandon could do nothing about the edge that entered his tone of voice.

"Oh, settle down. I'm not upset, just surprised. One of the reasons my ex walked out was because he thought Jessie was gay." She quickly turned toward Jessie. "Not that it was your fault in any way shape or form—and good riddance to bad rubbish. If you are or aren't makes no difference to me. You know you can talk to me about anything. Right, Jessie?"

Jessie looked horrified for a moment and shot a quick look around to see who was within hearing distance, before blurting out, "I *am* gay, Mom."

Meghan nodded decisively. "I thought so. Glad the big reveal is out of the way. Now, come give me a hug before you go join your team."

Jessie walked to his mom and gave her a quick hug before turning and making his way across the field with Jeremy. Jeremy's voice trailed back to them. "See, Jess? I told you that you had nothing to worry about."

"Yeah. You were right."

Meghan slumped into her chair. "Man, I didn't think he was ever going to admit that."

"Yeah? What made you think he was gay?"

"Well, let's see... The collection of pretty-boy posters on his walls, regardless of his sporting prowess."

"A lot of the players are pretty. There could be a logical explanation."

"The makeup I found stashed under his bathroom sink when I was looking for the extra cleaning supplies…"

"He could have been holding it for a friend."

"Or, I know, how about the online searches about how to have gay sex."

"That one is a little harder to explain away."

"Lordy, I really hope he isn't having sex yet."

"I don't think he is. I don't get the impression either of our boys are at that stage yet. Probably just curiosity at this point."

Brandon saw Meghan giving him the side-eye. "What?"

"Do you think you could give Jessie the sex talk?"

Brandon dropped his mouth open.

"I don't want to tell him the wrong things, and he respects you. I mean, I can do research, but *gah*."

Brandon thought for a moment. "How about we both give them the sex talk to make sure we cover all the bases. Tag team it the whole way."

Meghan relaxed into her chair. "That would be awesome."

"All right then. It's a plan."

Nikolai was making his way across the field, and Brandon stood to meet him halfway. Nik was loaded down with a cooler and his chair, so Brandon reached out and took the chair to help. "I'm so happy to see you." He leaned in and gave Nik a quick peck on the lips. Nik looked stunned and raised his hand to his lips for a moment.

"Not that I'm complaining, but what brought that on?"

"Jessie just came out to his mother, and his mother asked me to give Jessie the gay-sex talk."

Nikolai started laughing as they finished crossing the field. "That's fantastic. What did you say?"

"I suggested we work together to give the talk to both boys at the same time."

"Good suggestion."

"Meghan, this is Nikolai Barinov. Nik, this is Jessie's mother, Meghan Paul."

"Pleased to meet you," Nikolai replied.

"Good to meet you as well, Nikolai. We were just talking about you."

"You were? Good things, I hope."

Meghan rocked her head from side to side. "Yes and no. All good things about you. Jeremy certainly sang your praises, but bad things about training Shawn so he could beat people up."

Nikolai winced. "Yeah, well, we do the best we can. Shawn is no longer training at our dojo, and as you know, he is in a lot of trouble at the moment. I spent a couple of hours talking to the police yesterday afternoon. It wasn't fun."

"I know that logically. It's the emotional response I'm struggling with." Meghan let out a huge sigh. "I do think it would be a good idea for Jessie to have lessons, so he can protect himself. I'm not sure it's in the budget right now, though."

"I can help. I'll get him the friends and family discount and maybe hold a class for Jeremy and Jessie. It won't hurt for Jeremy to know some things too."

"True," Brandon agreed. "That sounds like a great idea. We can work out the details later." Pointing out at the field, he added, "The game is about to start."

At halftime, a voice called out, "Uncle Nik!"

Sergei's younger brother Sasha pulled Nikolai into a hug. Brandon stood to greet Sasha and was surprised when he was also pulled into a hug. He quickly hugged him back then watched in bemusement as Sasha switched to Russian and was obviously telling Nikolai an epic story, if the waving hands and excited tone were anything to go by. Nikolai laughed and pulled Sasha into another quick hug.

"English, Sasha. The others don't understand."

Sasha sent Brandon and Meghan a chagrined look. "Sorry, Brandon, Mrs. P."

"Wait! You know Jessie's mom?"

"Yeah. Jessie and I are in theater class together. He's really good. We've also played soccer against each other."

"Do you know my brother Jeremy then?" Brandon waved a hand at the bench where Jeremy and his team were sitting, getting some sort of instruction from the coach.

"Jeremy Whitaker is your brother? Why didn't I know that?"

Nikolai shot Brandon a grin. "You know our Brandon likes to keep things close to his vest."

Brandon flushed a little. "Well, it's not a secret anymore. Sergei found out and has already met him."

"Why would Jeremy have been a secret?" Meghan asked.

Before Brandon could come up with a response for Meghan, Nikolai jumped in. "He was a single parent going to work for Sergei Barinov. He didn't want Sergei to have any reason to think he couldn't do the job."

"But Sergei Barinov has the reputation of being one of the most flexible people to work for because his motto is 'family first'." Meghan looked truly perplexed by the idea that Brandon should have been concerned.

"I was newly out of college and had just gotten custody of Jeremy. I didn't know that at first, then didn't know how to bring it up." Brandon ended with a shrug.

Meghan nodded. "I get that. It's like dating. You don't know when you should bring up that you have a kid."

"Well, Brandon here solved that problem by not dating at all, until now."

Sasha's head whipped around to stare at Nikolai. "Wait! Are you dating Brandon now?"

"Yep."

"That's why you're here?"

"Yep."

"Wow. I can't wait to tell Jessie that being a dork can actually work when trying to get someone's attention. He'll be pleased." Someone yelled Sasha's name. "Gotta go. My game is next on field six if you want to come watch. The rest of the fam is there. I just wanted to check on Jessie."

"We'll come over after Jeremy's game so you can say hello."

"Thanks, Mrs. P. See you soon." With a last hug for Nikolai, Sasha started loping over to field six.

"And that was my cousin Sasha. That boy is like a whirlwind."

"You should hear when Jeremy, Sasha and Jessie get going in a conversation. It's like a hornet's nest of energy," Meghan added.

"I wonder if Jeremy realizes who Sasha is? I've never heard him talk about him." Brandon pondered out loud.

"Everyone calls him Bones, if that helps," Meghan replied.

"Sasha is Bones?" Brandon scrunched his nose in confusion. "Why?"

"He's a huge *Star Trek* fan," Nikolai said with a shrug. "So that makes sense."

"What do bones have to do with *Star Trek*?"

Nikolai and Meghan both gave him looks of horror. "Have you not ever watched *Star Trek*?" Nikolai stuttered out.

"No. I haven't had a lot of spare time for television."

"That is just sad. We need to fix that. Stat."

"Let me guess. You're a huge *Star Trek* fan too."

"Where do you think Sasha got it from? *Star Trek*. The Marvel universe. It's all amazing."

"I have watched some of the Marvel movies. Jeremy loves them."

"Okay then, at least we aren't starting from scratch. The game's getting ready to start again. Let's see if Jeremy's team can make a comeback."

"They're only down by one. It's doable."

"They're lucky to only be down by one with the way they're playing."

"Yeah. Their goalie also plays on a travel team and is being scouted by some colleges."

"I can see that. Sasha could be that good, but he doesn't have the drive to do it. He prefers the theater and stuff."

"Jessie loves the game but doesn't have the skills to be really good," Meghan added with a grin. "At least it gets us both out of the house and there aren't a ton of equipment costs."

"Yeah. It's better than most organized sports," Nikolai agreed.

"Maybe that's something we should think about for the center. Fundraising for equipment for low-income families. If the children have the drive, it could be a way out for them."

"Hm-m, maybe. That might be a better fit for Saul and Eric, though." Turning to Meghan, he clarified. "Our friends Eric and Saul own V & H Sporting Goods. They were talking last week about trying to figure out another way to give back. This might be a really good idea for them."

"Yeah. You're right, Nik. I'll call them Monday then let them think about doing it, maybe in conjunction with the center."

"What's this center you guys keep mentioning?"

The rest of the game was spent alternately watching the game, cheering the boys on and talking about the idea behind the center. After the final whistle, they stood and folded their chairs while waiting for the boys to make it back. Final score had been three to two, so it was a decent showing even though still a loss.

"Hey, Brandon, was that Bones I saw talking to you at halftime?" Jeremy asked.

"Yep. Did you know he's Sergei's younger brother?"

"Really? No, I didn't. Did you know, Jessie?"

"Yeah. Bones talks about his brother all the time – and he's been to a few of our shows."

"Huh. My brother works for his brother then. Cool."

"Yep, and he wants you guys to come over to field six so he can see for himself how Jessie is doing."

Meghan pointed behind them. "He's on field six. Let's go say hello, then I think it's time to get you out of the sun for a bit. You're looking a little worn out, my son."

"Yeah, I'm feeling it a little too. Can Jeremy still come over?"

"Sure. Are you guys going to stay for Bones' game?"

"I probably should as long as we're here. I'll never hear the end of it if I don't. You don't have to stay though, Brandon, if you don't want to."

"If Jeremy's going with Jessie, I'll stay, then maybe we can get some dinner before I go pick up Jeremy. What time do I need to get him by, Meghan?"

"Let's say seven. That will give me time to at least feed him his first dinner, tonight."

"First dinner?" Nikolai asked, obviously confused.

"Yeah. Jeremy is constantly eating. If he eats dinner at five or six, you can almost guarantee he will want another whole meal at some point around nine. He is a bottomless pit, but he has also grown about six inches this year, so I guess there's a reason for it."

"I don't think I hit a six-inch growth spurt ever. I kept hoping, but it never happened."

"Well, I think you're perfect the way you are," Brandon said without pausing to think about what he was saying. His cheeks heated again, and he tried to cover it, by turning to pick up his chair. "Um-m, come on. Let's head to the other field. We have about ten minutes before the next set of games start. Hopefully, Sasha can take a minute and talk to Jessie so he can see he's okay."

Nikolai joined them, slid his hand into Brandon's and gave it a quick squeeze before letting go again. "I think you're perfect the way you are too." Nikolai kissed him on the cheek then turned and walked away. Brandon ignored the thumbs-up sign he received from each of the teenagers and turned to follow Nikolai.

Brandon greeted Sergei and Sasha's mother and father, Daria and Sean Hamilton, before turning to greet Sergei and Stuart. "Hey, guys. I didn't know you were going to be here today."

"We didn't know, either," Stuart answered as he stood up to shake Brandon's hand. "Sasha called us about an hour ago to ask us to come. Daria wants us to go for dinner afterward. So, we will be well compensated for our time."

"You boys should come too," Daria said as she released Nikolai from a hug and came to give Brandon his.

Brandon shared a look with Nikolai before turning back and responding. "We must decline today. Nikolai and I are going out for our first date after the game. I hope you understand, ma'am."

"Wait! What? You and Nikolai? When did this happen? Never mind. You said 'first date' so it must be new. I'm so excited. Two of my favorite people together."

"Thank you, ma'am."

Daria swatted Brandon on the shoulder. "How many times have I asked you not to ma'am me. It's either Daria or Mama H, as Nikolai calls me."

"Yes, ma'am. I mean Mama H?" Brandon shot another quick glance to Nikolai to find him grinning back.

"Yes. Mama H. We don't want our future children to be confused, now do we?"

Brandon's jaw dropped for the second time before he caught Nikolai's smirk. "One step at a time there, speed demon. Let's see if you can manage to date me without causing yourself any more bodily injury first."

"Ha-ha. I'm over it." Nikolai's words were accompanied by an airy wave of the hand.

"Wasn't it just last week...?" Sergei said with a grin.

"Shut it, Sergei. This conversation doesn't involve you."

"But?"

"Zip it, Barinov, or I will get even."

Sergei crossed his arms over his broad chest. "Mama, you hear Nikolai threatening me, don't you?"

"Yes. And I also hear that you deserve it. Leave poor Nikolai alone."

"Poor Nikolai?"

"Yes. Nikolai didn't give you a hard time when you were moping over not being able to talk to Stuart during the investigation into your sister's former boyfriend. You should show him the same courtesy." Nikolai opened his mouth to say something, only to have Daria stab a finger in his direction. "And you... You should let your family know your challenges, accomplishments and achievements. What is this I hear about you being a black belt? Why would you not tell us about that?"

Nikolai shrugged. "Because it was mine. It wasn't a 'Barinov' thing. It was a 'Nik' thing, not even a 'Nikolai' thing. I'm just 'Nik' there. All successes and failures were mine and mine alone."

Daria looked at him with stark assessment for a few moments, before sharply nodding her head. "I can understand that."

"What? How? That doesn't make sense. Everything he does is his!"

"Sergei, son, I love you. You know I do, but you *do* have a tendency to butt your nose in where it doesn't belong. I can understand Nikolai wanting something that didn't touch or involve you in any way."

Brandon chuckled at Sergei's true confusion at the thought of him not being involved in something that affected the people in his life. "Just let him do his thing, Bossman. It's all good."

Sergei looked at Stuart for obvious guidance. "I'll explain it all to you later, babe. Let's watch the game."

Jeremy bounced back up beside Brandon. "Hey, Brandon, I'm going to head out with Jessie and his mom now."

"First meet Sergei's parents, then you can go. Mama H and Sean, I would like you to meet my brother, Jeremy. Jeremy, Daria and Sean Hamilton."

"I've actually met them before, when we stopped to pick Bones up one time. It's nice to see you again, Mr. and Mrs. Hamilton."

"Ah, I didn't realize you were related to our Brandon. You may call me Mama H as well."

A huge grin spread across Jeremy's face. "Great. Thank you."

"And why don't you call me Uncle Sergei," Sergei added with a shrug. "And him Uncle Stuart." With a thumb pointed in Stuart's direction.

"Wow. Suddenly we have all sorts of family, Brandon. This is great."

"You ready to go, Jeremy? I'm getting a little tired and sore. Mom's waiting in the car."

"Yep. Sorry, Jessie. I was just checking in with my brother and the Hamiltons. Text me when you're on your way to pick me up. Okay, Brandon?"

"Will do. I'll see you later."

"Have fun on your date."

"We will," Nikolai answered. "Thanks, Jeremy."

With a final wave, the boys headed off to the parking lot.

Chapter Seven

Nikolai had a hard time focusing on the game. It had been easier at the last match, since Meghan had been there as a kind of chaperone. He wasn't sure how he should act with Brandon in front of his family and Brandon's boss. He'd never actually introduced anyone he was dating to his family. Honestly, he'd been so busy with school that dating had kind of fallen by the wayside. He had no guideline here. *Is it okay to hold his hand? Should I keep a foot of space between us at all times? Should I ask those pesky 'getting to know you' questions or wait until dinner?*

Nikolai jumped when Brandon reached out and took his hand. Leaning in, he whispered in Nikolai's ear. "What's wrong?"

"Nothing." Nikolai sighed deeply when Brandon gave him a disbelieving look. "Really. Nothing's wrong. I just don't know how to act. I don't want to embarrass you."

Brandon snorted at him. "Why would you think anything you did would embarrass me?"

Nikolai lifted one shoulder in a half-shrug. "Let's just say that it has been my experience that people find me to be a bit much."

"Just relax and be yourself. I mean, you already have our future children calling your Aunt Daria, Mama H, after all."

"Do you want children?"

"Yeah. I would love to have the whole package one day — a husband, kid or kids, all of it."

Something relaxed inside Nikolai. "That's my dream, actually, and if I'm being completely honest, most of my fantasies about it have involved you for the last couple of years."

Brandon looked contrite for a moment. "I can't say the same thing. I've been trying really hard not to notice you, because I had this idea in my head that I needed to focus on work and Jeremy only. When I was suing for custody, I was so terrified that something would go wrong with the petition. Then I was terrified something was going to go wrong with the adoption, and that the courts would find some reason to deny it. The sad thing is I've recently realized that I'm still waiting for something to go wrong — but that's no way to live."

"No. It's not, but I can relate in a way, except mine was school. I'm a five-foot-seven, blond-haired, blue eyed, gender-fluid-dressing gay boy. I had to fight to be taken seriously while staying true to myself."

"Yeah. Well, I respect the hell out of you. You are one of the smartest people I know, and I love being around you. I decided I don't want to keep resisting the dream of you in my life."

"Aw," Sergei interrupted, "that's so sweet. Gag. Watch the game now. Flirt later."

Nikolai turned and laughed at his cousin. "Like you can talk. You and Stuart are a walking billboard of googly-eyed love."

Sergei crossed his arms over his chest and gave Nikolai a glare. "I have never had googly-eyes in my life."

Everyone in the group burst into laughter. Daria was the first to recover. "Oh, my sweet boy, you have nothing but googly-eyes for your Stuart. It is how I knew he was the one. You get this look on your face whenever you even talk about him."

"You melt like butter whenever you're talking to him," Nikolai added.

Sergei huffed in indignation and opened his mouth to reply, pausing when Stuart laid his hand on his arm. "I like it when you melt like butter, and I love the way you look at me."

Everyone started laughing again when Sergei completely deflated as he looked at Stuart. "Yeah. Yeah. Laugh it up. Just watch the game."

Nikolai glanced at Brandon to find him staring at him. "What?"

"I love to see you happy."

Nikolai's cheeks heated as he ducked his head to stare at their entwined fingers for a moment until he had himself under control. Looking up, he still found Brandon's gaze on him. "What?"

"How about we shelve any further discussion until dinner. Let's just enjoy this beginning."

Brandon raised Nikolai's hand to his mouth and kissed the back of it, causing Nikolai's stomach to flutter with what felt like a million butterflies, before Brandon lowered their joined hands to his thigh. "Sounds like a plan to me."

Nikolai kind of drifted through the rest of the game, simply enjoying hanging out with all the important people in his life. After consoling Sasha for his teams' three-to-nothing loss, Nikolai and Brandon made their way to the parking lot.

"Where do you want to eat?"

"I'm not picky," Brandon answered with a shrug. "Just somewhere we can talk is my only criteria."

Nikolai hesitated for a moment. "Do you want to come back with me to my apartment? We can order something, and it would give us a chance to talk uninterrupted."

"That sounds great. It's a fantastic day, weather-wise. Maybe we could eat on your roof terrace?"

"It is definitely a perfect day for it. Let's do that."

Nikolai had time on the ride to his place to second and third guess his suggestion. *Did I make my bed? Does it matter if I made my bed? Do I have dirty dishes in the sink? Oh shit. I definitely have a mess in my bedroom.* He had taken forever to decide what to wear today, leaving the rejected clothing on his bed. "First date, Barinov. He's not going to see your bedroom. This is simply dinner and conversation."

Nikolai pulled into his parking spot to the side of the building after using the gate opener Kirk had installed after Lee was attacked by his brother closing the gate one evening after hours. He was very thankful he didn't have to get out of his car to do so, especially late at night. He pressed the button again to close the gate after Brandon pulled into the spot next to him.

Nikolai got out then led the way up the stairs to the apartment above the garage. He unobtrusively wiped his hands on his pants before grabbing his keys out of his pocket.

"Why are you nervous? We don't have to have the date here if you don't want."

"I do want. It's just...I've never actually had anyone in my space here, and you're important. I don't want to mess this up now that you are finally giving me a chance."

Brandon reached out and cupped Nikolai's chin in his hand. "I should have done it a long time ago. As I said earlier, I got in my own way. I think we could have something really great."

"Me too," Nikolai whispered.

Brandon leaned in and placed a gentle kiss on Nikolai's lips before pulling back. "Now. Show me your place. I swear to you that your privacy and secrets are safe with me."

Nikolai tore his gaze from Brandon's lips, took a deep breath and turned his attention to opening the door. He stepped inside and heard Brandon gasp from behind him. Looking back, he watched as Brandon looked around his living room.

"It's amazing. It's bold and colorful, just like you. I mean, I didn't even know they made purple couches."

Nikolai couldn't help his chuckle. "Someone probably does, but I recovered this one. It's an old couch, and I probably should have tossed it, but I couldn't bear to do it because it's so comfortable."

"I'm that way with my office chair at home. It has duct tape in random places, but it's broken in just right. Seriously though, this is amazing. I love all the color in here, and it seems so you."

"Not too much?"

"Color? Nope. It's perfect. I'm a bit of a neat freak, as my brother told all of you, but you aren't messy.

Everything has its place here. It's like getting a Nikolai hug as soon as you walk in."

Nikolai's cheeks hurt because he was smiling so big. "Thank you for getting it. It means a lot to me that you do."

Brandon walked up and looked into his eyes. "I know you, Nikolai. Just because I was trying not to obsess about you doesn't mean I didn't watch you every chance I got."

Nikolai stepped into Brandon's space and wrapped his arms around him. "Are you telling me I had a stalker all this time, and I didn't realize?"

Brandon lifted his own arms and hugged Nikolai. "Yep, but at least I didn't walk into any doors."

Nikolai dropped his forehead to Brandon's chest and groaned. "Don't remind me. Not my finest moment."

"Or how about the time you were watching me instead of where you were going and fell into Kirk and Eric's pool fully clothed at their barbecue that one weekend?"

"Enough." Nikolai raised his head to rest his chin on Brandon's chest and look up at him. "Let's just agree that I'm a total dork for you and forget about all the stupid things I did."

Brandon leaned down to peck another kiss to Nikolai's lips. "I'm not going to forget, but I will stop giving you a hard time about them — even though they are some of my fondest memories of you."

"Perhaps we should work on making better memories to replace them?"

"What did you have in mind?"

Nikolai went up on his tiptoes so he could press his lips to Brandon's. He was gratified when Brandon quickly got with the program and tightened his arms around Nikolai to pull their bodies flush together. Nikolai moaned into the kiss, opening his mouth to allow Brandon's tongue entrance. Nikolai had never been kissed so thoroughly in his life. *Is this what they always talk about in romance books? The overwhelming kiss?*

Nikolai grumbled in protest when Brandon pulled away to rest their foreheads together. They breathed in sync for a few moments, and Brandon ran his hands up and down Nikolai's back.

"Damn, I want you," Brandon rasped.

"I want you too. So much," Nikolai whispered back.

"I want to try to do this right, though. No sex on the first date. Plus, we only have a few hours before I have to go pick up Jeremy. I want to be able to take my time with you."

"I know you're right." Nikolai shuddered when Brandon made it to his ass and gently cupped both cheeks. "That's not fair. Hands above the waist, Whitaker."

Brandon gave a squeeze before moving his hands to Nikolai's waist and pushing him back, creating some space between them. "Sorry...not sorry."

Nikolai pointed a finger at him. "That wicked smirk isn't fair, either. You are way too sexy for my own good."

Brandon's grin kicked up another notch, before he leaned in and whispered in Nikolai's ear. "Oh, I can be very good for you, baby."

Nikolai shuddered then slapped his chest lightly and stepped back. "None of that. We are being good and having a get-to-know-each-other date. Now what do you want to order to eat? Any allergies I need to be concerned about?"

"Nope. Neither Jeremy nor I have any food allergies, for future reference."

"Great. How about we order from my favorite Chinese place then? I've been craving some moo shu pork and egg rolls. Oh, and wonton soup."

"Sounds great. Egg drop soup for me, though."

"Ew. Egg drop soup is just slimy."

"And moo shu isn't?"

"Different kind of slimy and it has crunchy bits."

Brandon burst out laughing. "All righty then. I'll remember not to kiss you after eating egg drop soup, but I still want it."

Nikolai gave a large put-upon sigh. "I'll order it if I must."

"You must."

"Is one order of moo shu enough or did you want to order a second dish?"

"I wouldn't say no to sweet and sour chicken. Leftovers are always good."

"Sounds like a plan. There are drinks in the mini-fridge upstairs on the terrace in the outdoor kitchen if you want to head on up." Nikolai pulled out his phone and looked for the saved number for the restaurant in his contacts. He placed the order then followed Brandon up the stairs. He found him in the hammock Nikolai had set up. He loved to lay in it and read or lay in it at night when the stars started coming out. "Forty-five minutes is the estimate."

"Great. Come join me. This hammock holds two, right?"

"It's supposed to."

"I didn't know what you wanted to drink."

"I'm good for now. I'll grab something when the food gets here."

Nikolai gently climbed into the hammock and gravity had him sliding into Brandon. Brandon wrapped his arm around him and pulled him in for a snuggle. Nikolai lowered his head to Brandon's chest with a sigh, wrapping his own arm around Brandon's waist.

"You are quite comfy, kind sir."

Nikolai felt more than heard Brandon's chuckle. "Glad you think so. I love to cuddle."

"Me too." Nikolai closed his eyes and allowed himself to relax and just be — something he didn't let himself do that often. It was nice. A buzz from his phone roused him a bit later. Glancing at the screen, he saw that the delivery driver was almost there. "Food's here. I need to get up."

"Okay."

Nikolai almost flipped himself on his face trying to get out of the hammock. He put his hand down to catch himself just in time. Bringing his feet around so he could stand, he glanced back at Brandon to see him shaking his head.

"What? Hammocks are notoriously difficult to get out of. I was trying to be nice and not rock you completely out of it."

"Uh-huh. Okay. Let's go with that. Thank you, Nikolai, for saving my life."

"That's more like it. At least wait until I get to the stairs before you start laughing, okay?"

Brandon pressed his lips together in an obvious attempt to hide his smile, and slowly nodded his head. Nikolai straightened his clothes as he made the walk to the stairs and down. The echo of Brandon's soft laughter followed him, making him grin.

Chapter Eight

Brandon sat back in his chair at the patio table with a groan. "I am so full. You're right. That is some of the best Chinese food I have ever had."

"Told you. Trust me. I know all the best food places."

"And yet you don't have an ounce of fat on you."

"Well, I work out a lot. I'm at the dojo at least three, usually four days a week, if not more."

"Yeah. About that. How did you keep that from Sergei?"

Nikolai chuckled. "I don't know if you've realized this about your boss and my dear cousin, but he has a rather large case of tunnel-vision and is a bit self-absorbed. His projects are generally all for the betterment of other people, but if it doesn't involve one of his projects — or his mother and siblings or now Stuart — it doesn't make it on his radar too much. He is the best guy and loves with his entire soul, but he doesn't really think people have a life outside of his interaction with them. Case in point…how did he not know about your brother?"

Brandon shrugged. "As you said, it wasn't that hard to keep it quiet. Sergei didn't seem to realize I had a life other than the job. It's only now that he has Stuart and has started to pay attention to more than his company that the thought would even have occurred to him." Brandon paused for a moment. "That's not the whole story, either. It's only recently I have felt comfortable telling him, now that the company isn't his entire world. Don't get me wrong. I know he values me and my skills, but until Stuart, a small part of me was worried that he would find someone else. Before you say anything, I knew it wasn't right. Sergei at his core is a great guy."

Nikolai reached out and took Brandon's hand in his, idly playing with his fingers. "I can understand your fears. It's like my being gay. I was going to the dojo for five years, before I even mentioned it to Sensei. I knew he wouldn't care. He talked about his brother and his brother's partner then husband all the time, but I couldn't ever seem to be able to say the words." Nikolai chuckled. "When I finally did say something, Sensei was like 'thank goddess you finally admitted it. I was thinking of putting a Pride flag in my office, so you would maybe spit it out already'."

Nikolai looked up, and Brandon was struck by the gorgeousness of Nikolai's blue eyes. They were almost sapphire in color today. He had to force himself to pay attention to what Nikolai said next.

"I bought Sensei two Pride flags for his birthday — one for outside the dojo and one for his office. He laughed and said they were perfect, then he made me help him put them up. That was a good day. He lost a few students but gained a bunch more, so it all worked out."

"Yeah well, I think Sergei has adopted Jeremy at this point. It's insane."

"Yep. Sergei and his family are crazy, but it's a good crazy."

Brandon winced. "My family is kind of the bad crazy, so I'm happy to be a part of yours now."

"Was it just your mom? No grandparents or aunts and uncles?"

"I have both an aunt and an uncle, as well as grandparents somewhere. My father's family. Mom said they were super religious and didn't like that he married a Hispanic woman."

"So, you take after your mother then?"

"Coloring-wise yeah. I'm the spitting image of my father in every other way, though."

"I can see why your mother fell for him then. You are very hot, Mr. Whitaker."

Brandon chuckled. "Thank you. Anyway, my parents met in college. My dad was studying criminal justice after he'd served four years in the military, so he was a little older. My mom was studying psychology. There was some degree program overlap, so they had a class together. From the way my mom tells it, it was love at first sight. Of course, she usually told the story when she was drunk, so I don't know how accurate it was."

"From what you remember of them together, were they happy?"

"So happy. Some of my earliest memories are of them dancing together in the living room. They were so in love."

"And your grandparents couldn't see that?"

"Nope. I guess all they could see was the color of her skin. Supposedly, they questioned her citizenship status and told my father she only wanted to marry him to get a green card. My mother is a third-generation US citizen, the first to go to college. Her parents were so proud of her."

"What about your mother's family then?"

"She was an only child. Her parents were older when they had her. They died when I was three, I think—first my grandmother then my grandfather six months later. Ironically, only her parents were supportive of her marrying my father, because he was not only white, but also a cop to boot. My mom came from a different part of the state but stayed here after college to be with my father, since he was lucky enough to get a job here. They wouldn't answer her calls anymore after her parents died."

"What a mess."

"Yep."

"But now you've got us."

Brandon looked down at their entwined fingers for a moment before looking back at Nikolai. "I think the only member of your family I would need to truly be happy is you. The rest are just wonderful icing on the cake. I was stunned the first time I saw you. You took my breath away, and I haven't been able to catch it since. You thought I was judging you, but I never knew quite what to say to you."

"That's how I felt about you, too. It was like being struck by lightning." Nikolai gave a self-deprecating laugh. "At least you didn't trip and spill coffee all over Sergei when you saw me for the first time."

"That was pretty epic. I thought we weren't going to talk about it anymore, though?"

"True. Subject change. I'm glad Jeremy doesn't have a problem with us dating. He seems like a great kid."

"He has his moments. He is a stereotypical teenager, so there is drama from time to time — and not all of it is in the theater."

"Oh, I remember those days. What do you do with him when you have to go out of town?"

"Until recently, Sergei was the one who went out of town, and I manned the fort here in Raleigh. The last couple of trips have been a combination of my next-door neighbor, Mr. Gonzalez, and Jessie's house. Jeremy is pretty self-sufficient now, so if it's just an overnight, he's usually okay."

"It's good that you have a nice neighbor who will do that for you."

"It's a two-way street. Mr. Gonzalez is getting up there in age. He keeps an eye on Jeremy if I have to work late or whatever. In return, Jeremy and I take care of his yardwork and any minor repairs and things for him."

"Sounds like a win-win to me."

"It is."

"So" — Nikolai cleared his throat — "are we really going to do this?"

"This?"

"Date. Be a couple."

"Thought we covered that already. Yes. I want to date you. Yes. I consider us a couple and before you ask, date exclusively."

Nikolai looked up at him through his lashes. "And you'll tell me if I get to be too much? You won't just disappear, right?"

"Did someone do that to you?"

"Most people do that to me. I'm a lot."

"Not to me you're not. You're perfect."

"Ha. You say that now…"

"I say that now and I will say that fifty years from now. You are amazing."

"But you'll tell me if I do something that's too much?"

Brandon reached across the table and gently framed Nikolai's face with his hands, forcing Nik to look at him. "You just need to be you. That's it. Whoever you want to be. However you want to dress. Be Nikolai."

Nikolai searched Brandon's eyes. Brandon supposed he was trying to see how sincere he was. Swallowing hard, he leaned forward and kissed Brandon's lips. "Thank you. You'll talk to Jeremy too, though? I want him to like me."

"Jeremy is very laid back. He'll be fine. I want you happy. If that means you wear a hoop skirt and a sombrero, so be it." He paused for a second. "Although either item might make it difficult for me to kiss or hug you, so I would prefer you didn't."

Nikolai snorted a laugh. "That would be a little much as a fashion statement, even for me. I don't think I'm tall enough to pull off something like that."

"If anyone could do it, you could."

"Aw, you say the sweetest things." Nikolai paused and looked at his phone. "It's six-thirty. I know you have to go in a few minutes."

"Yeah. I need to get Jeremy home and make sure he's ready for school tomorrow. I've had fun, though."

"Me too."

"Let me help you clean up the mess before I head out."

Nikolai nodded then stood to collect all the trash into the bag it had come in then stacked the leftovers neatly to carry downstairs. Brandon collected their dirty silverware, glasses and plates and followed Nikolai to the kitchen, where he put the items in the dishwasher. He washed his hands at the sink before making room for Nikolai to do the same. Brandon leaned back against the counter next to the sink so he could simply look at Nikolai.

"What? Do I have something on my face?"

"Not at all. You're gorgeous — and I like looking at you."

Nikolai shut off the water and turned to take the dishtowel from Brandon. Brandon didn't let the towel go, though, and used it to yank Nikolai closer then wrapped his arms around him to pull him tight.

"Oh."

Brandon waited until Nikolai looked up at him before swooping in for a kiss. He took advantage of Nikolai's startled gasp to sweep his tongue into Nikolai's mouth. Brandon could taste the moo shu and sweet and sour that they had just consumed. Underlying all of that was the wonderful flavor of Nikolai — spicy and strong and maybe he was getting a little too poetic, but it was necessary. He could truly get addicted to kissing Nikolai. He eased back when the alarm on his phone went off.

"I have to go."

"Yeah."

Nikolai stepped away then started chuckling.

"What?"

"You have wet handprints on your chest. I hope they dry before you pick up your brother. It looks like I groped you."

Brandon glanced down to see that he did indeed have handprints on his shirt. "You did grope me."

"I did—and I enjoyed it, too." Nikolai ended his statement with a saucy wink. "Now come on. Let me walk you to the door."

Another long kiss later, and Brandon skipped down the stairs to his car. He texted Jeremy to let him know he was on his way before starting the engine. Nikolai was able to open the gate from his apartment, and Brandon gave him a final wave as he pulled through. Seeing Nikolai blow him a kiss in return made him happier than he had been in a long time.

He was still smiling when he picked up his brother a few minutes later. A quick glance down as he walked to the door at Jessie's house showed that the handprints were gone. He was strangely disappointed.

The door opened before he got a chance to think about it anymore, and his brother came out, closing the door behind him. He turned around and started to retrace his steps to the car, as his brother bounced up beside him.

"Yo, Bran. How'd it go?"

"It went well. We had a good time."

"Great. I'm glad. Nik seems like a good guy."

"He really is. Do you have everything?"

"Yep. Didn't bring much."

"Is your homework done?"

"I have to study for a science test tomorrow that Jessie just reminded me about, but everything else is done."

Brandon waited until they were both in the car and heading home before continuing the conversation. "Listen. Nikolai is a little worried about you being weirded out if he wears a dress or something around you. I told him you wouldn't care, but I just wanted to check in with you, warn you. Hell, I don't know." Jeremy turned to stare at him. "What?"

"Why do I care what Nikolai wears?"

"I don't know. Because you're a teenager, and he doesn't want to embarrass you?"

"Nah. It's all cool. Ned Jones became Stacey last year. My friend Lex dresses according to her mood that day."

"Well, Nikolai doesn't want to be a female. He just doesn't differentiate between male and female clothing. He wears what he feels like."

"Good for him."

"Yeah?"

"Yeah. It's all good. It's just clothes. I don't see what the big deal is. I mean Jesus wore robes, right?"

"I guess that's one way of looking at it."

"Tell Nikolai not to worry."

"I already did, but he's still worried."

"Yeah. I get it. I'm sure he was given crap for it."

"Yep."

"He's got us now, though. We've got his back, bro."

Brandon shot his brother a smile. "Yes, we do."

Chapter Nine

Nikolai stared at the spreadsheet he was working on, not really seeing the numbers on the screen. Instead, he was thinking about his boyfriend of two weeks and the fact that they were having a sleepover…finally. The last two weeks had been a mix of conflicting and busy schedules. They had managed dinner alone one more night and dinner three times with Jeremy. Brandon had needed to work with Sergei through the previous weekend on the final takeover details of Trinity Corporation. Sergei made his move on Monday, so now it was simply a matter of following through.

He was surprisingly nervous about the night. His bag was packed, and he had his favorite undergarments laid out on his bed, ready to put on after his shower. They were feminine and lacey in a gorgeous sapphire blue that looked fantastic with his skin tone, even if he did say so himself. The matching camisole always made him feel fabulous. He wiggled in his seat then jumped when Lee's voice came from behind him.

"Hey, Nikolai. What's with the ants in your pants this evening?"

"Man, you scared the shit out of me. Make some noise next time, why don't you." He turned in his chair to see Lee raising an incredulous eyebrow at him. "Don't look at me with that judgy eyebrow!"

"I said your name three times, Nikolai. You were in your own little world."

"Sorry. I'm…"

"Fretting?"

"Men don't fret. We calculate odds and contingencies—and stop with the judgy eyebrow." Nikolai crossed his arms with a huff and sat back in his chair. "I finally get to, fingers crossed, spend the night with Brandon tonight and I'm nervous, okay?"

"Is Jeremy going to be at the house too?"

"No. Jeremy and Jessie are both spending the night at Sasha's to swim and practice their audition pieces for a play with a local theater group. Auditions are on Saturday afternoon. Brandon has strict instructions not to show up, because he makes Jeremy nervous for some reason. Mama H agreed to take them all to the audition then wants everyone to come over for a barbecue at their house afterward."

"And…?"

"And that means Brandon is mine for a solid twenty-four hours. I even handed off my Saturday classes at the dojo to Sensei."

"And…" This time it was accompanied by a rolling hand gesture. "That's what you want, right?"

"It really is, but I want everything to be perfect."

"I'm sure it will be," Lee said while grasping Nikolai's shoulder and giving it a squeeze."

Nikolai threw his hands into the air. "Have you seen me when I'm nervous around Brandon? I turn into the biggest dork. He'll be lucky to make it out alive!"

Lee pressed his lips together, probably in an attempt to hide his smile.

"Go ahead. Laugh at the man having a nervous breakdown." Nikolai got up to pace.

Lee stepped in Nikolai's path and put a hand on each of his shoulders, giving him a slight shake. "It will be fine, Nikolai. Brandon knows you and still wants you to come over. From what I've seen of the two of you together, your chemistry is off the charts. Just go and enjoy it. Don't put so much pressure on yourself."

"Have you met me?"

Lee winced at his screech.

"What's going on?" Kirk asked from his office door, causing both men to turn and look at him.

"Nik is having a nervous breakdown—his words—about spending the night with Brandon tonight."

"If you don't want to go…"

"Oh, he wants to go. He real-ly wants to go. He's worried he's going to screw it up."

"And he's right here, asshole."

Lee turned the judgy eyebrow on him again. This time Nikolai sagged in defeat. "I know. It will be fine, but keep your phone handy in case I need you, okay?"

"Why would you possibly need me?"

Nikolai threw his hands up in the air again. "I don't know."

Kirk came closer, and Nikolai stared up at him helplessly. "It'll all be fine, Nik. You've managed to have several meals with him now without injuring yourself. You'll have a great time."

"But we haven't been naked," Nik yelled as he heard the door chime behind him. He closed his eyes in horror. "I don't want to look. Who came in — and did they hear me?"

"Now who's getting naked?" The sound of a familiar New Jersey accent made Nikolai sag in relief before he spun to greet her.

"Hi, Gracie. What're you doing here?"

"Flew down special to have dinner with my favorite client and his gorgeous husband. Do you two want to join us? I would be the envy of all the women and probably most of the men to be surrounded by such amazing male specimens."

"Sorry, Gracie. Eric and I have dinner plans with his mom, and Nikolai has a hot date."

"Details. Details. Give me details." Gracie made grabby hands as she got closer then snagged Nikolai's face to pull him in for a fuchsia-colored-lipstick, smacking kiss, before leaning back and giving him a thorough once-over. "Oh, that shade of lipstick is fantastic on you. Look at him. So gorgeous. You're sure you're gay now?"

"My boyfriend sure hopes so, ma'am, and I think your boyfriend might be upset if that wasn't the case. And I'm sure you're here for more than having dinner with your favorite client, for that matter. How *is* Jeff, by the way?"

"Jeff knows he has nothing to worry about. The things that man can do with his tongue alone garner my complete devotion."

"TMI, Gracie," all three men said together.

"Whatever. Such prudes. Now stop changing the subject. Who is this boyfriend? What do we know about him? Is he good enough for our Nikolai?"

"You've met him, Gracie," Lee said as he leaned down for his own kiss. "Nik is dating Sergei's assistant, Brandon."

"Oh my. The two of you would be gorgeous together. I approve."

Nikolai couldn't help but laugh at the exuberant woman. "I'm glad you do."

"So, what's the problem?"

Lee answered before Nikolai could. "He's having his first sleepover and he's nervous."

"I'm not nervous about the sleepover. I want to go on the sleepover. I'm nervous about" — Nikolai paused when he remembered who he was talking to and finished lamely with — "other things."

"Oh well, if it's your first time, I'm sure one of these gentlemen will be happy to give you instructions."

Nikolai widened his eyes in horror as what she was saying sank in, and he started shaking his hands in front of him. "No. No. No. I know what to do. I've done it plenty. I mean, I'm not a whore or anything but enough to know what I'm doing in that department." Nikolai trailed off helplessly and covered his eyes with one hand in hopes of escaping the horror of this conversation. "Somebody shoot me now, please. Put me out of my misery."

That did it. Everyone erupted into laughter.

"Not. Funny."

"It so is," Lee choked out while wiping the tears from his face with one hand and clutching his stomach with the other. "The look on your face is priceless."

"Okay, Nikolai, I'm glad you don't need instruction," Kirk said through his chuckles. "Why don't you call it a day and go get ready? We've got it from here. Gracie, it's always a pleasure to see you, but

I have a few more things to take care of before I can leave today. Lee, are you done with the last car of the day?"

"Yep. Just need to wash up and grab my things, and I will be ready to go, Gracie. Give me five minutes."

"Take your time, sugar."

"Nik, we've got this. We only have one more customer due to pick up their car. I can handle it. Enjoy your weekend. Now *go!*"

"Thanks, Kirk. I'll see you Monday." Nik leaned down and placed a kiss on Gracie's cheek. Then he opened his mouth, realized he had no idea what to say, shook his head and walked toward the stairs with a wave. "Everyone, have a great weekend!"

"Bye, darling. Make sure you use lots of lube. That Brandon is a big boy, and I sure hope he's proportional."

"Gah." Nikolai sped up to get away from the too-helpful woman with the good heart, and his laughing hyena friends.

Nikolai felt better after a relaxing, hot shower, where he took the time to manscape and prep for the evening. Stepping into his chosen silky underwear and matching camisole, Nik ran his hands down his chest, enjoying the feel of the material against his skin. Turning to the outfit on the bed, he second-guessed his choice, or probably twelve-thousandth-guessed his choice would be more accurate, but ultimately decided to go with it.

The gauzy blouse-like white shirt showed hints of the blue cami underneath. The billowy shorts masquerading as a skirt stopped just above his knee. He finished the look with strappy sandals and a light application of makeup and put his hair up on top of his head in his usual messy bun. He gave a nod of approval to his reflection in the mirror before scooping up his overnight bag and heading out of the door.

Pulling up to the curb at Brandon's house, Nik took a minute to check it out since this was his first time there. The two-story house was well maintained, as was the house to its left, which must be Mr. Gonzalez' house, because they had matching immaculate lawns, unlike the house on the right with the foot-high weeds. Brandon's house had a welcoming front porch that contained a couple of rocking chairs, perfect for relaxing on after a hard day. While it was obviously part of a community built by one builder, Brandon had obviously done his best to put his stamp on his.

Nikolai stepped out of the car and, after grabbing his overnight bag, started up the sidewalk. The front door opened before he made it to the porch, and he smiled up at Brandon. "Were you watching for me?"

"I was." His gaze took a slow path down then back up Nikolai's body. "You look fantastic."

A wave of heat rolled through Nikolai at the want in Brandon's voice and eyes. He walked up the steps and into Brandon's arms. "I'm glad you like it."

Brandon wrapped one arm around Nikolai's back and snuck the other under his shirt to rub his fingers against the silk at Nikolai's waist, before bending his head and taking Nikolai's mouth in a hungry kiss.

"Not that I don't appreciate the view, but maybe you young-un's should take that inside," a voice called from next door. They pulled apart with a gasp, and Nikolai buried his face in Brandon's shoulder in embarrassment.

Brandon ran both hands down Nikolai's back in a soothing gesture. "Jealous, old man?"

"Yep. I thought your boyfriend was coming over. You should probably get this girl on her way if you don't want to upset him."

Nikolai's embarrassment turned to amusement. He stood up straight and turned toward the voice. "Hello. You must be Mr. Gonzalez. I've heard a lot about you. You are correct. His boyfriend would be very upset if he were kissing a girl, but since I'm the boyfriend, it's all good."

A low whistle rang out. "Damn, boy, you got yourself a looker."

Nikolai swung his pointer finger between himself and Brandon. "Which one of us?"

There was a long pause. "Both actually, but don't tell Brandon I said so. His head's big enough. He's been strutting around like a tom cat since he finally got his head out of his ass and asked you out."

"Well, I, for one, am glad he did."

"Me too. Now I know you have a date, so go have some fun. I'll put on my noise-cancelling headphones when I go to bed. Don't worry about disturbing me." With a wave, Mr. Gonzalez went into his house and shut the door.

Nikolai started laughing and laughed harder when he looked at Brandon and saw the pink tint on his cheeks. "Was he waiting just to check me out?"

"Yep. Nosy old bugger."

"That's awesome. He's amazing."

"He has his moments."

"Did he know it was me the whole time?"

"Yes. We've talked about how you dress, and he probably watched you from the minute you pulled up to the curb. That was his way of saying welcome."

"I love it."

"Yeah. He's a great guy, if you can get past his warped sense of humor."

"In other words, he fits right in."

Brandon's grin was huge. "Pretty much. Let's go in, so we don't give him anything else to harass us about."

Nikolai followed Brandon into the house and looked around with interest at the living room. "Jeremy already gone?"

"Yep. Dropped him off a half-hour ago. He's pretty nervous about his audition."

"Hasn't he done it before?"

"Nope. It's been Jessie's thing. Jessie talked him into auditioning with him this time, though. Jeremy, Jessie and Sasha aka Bones have gotten pretty tight, even though Bones is older than them. Sasha is a good kid. I guess there's going to be a whole group there tomorrow at the barbecue."

"That should be fun."

"Yep. Now…what are you feeling for dinner? We could go out, order in or stay in and make something. Your choice."

"Well, let's start with the appetizers then we'll decide."

"What appetize…er?" Nikolai plastered himself to Brandon's front and leaned up for a kiss. "Oh, that appetizer. I love that appetizer."

"Stop talking, Brandon, and show me your bedroom."

"Yes, sir."

Nikolai took one last kiss before stepping back and allowing Brandon to take the lead up the stairs. Nikolai was so busy watching Brandon's ass flex in his jeans as he climbed that he missed a step and only managed to catch himself on the banister at the last second. Brandon glanced back in concern.

"Are you okay?"

"Yep. Nothing to see here. Carry on."

Luckily, there were only a few steps left, and Nikolai was able to focus long enough to make it safely. He peered around the bedroom space with interest. It was very Brandon. He had a sleek sleigh bed in warm colors, with drawers underneath for his storage needs, but it was covered in lots of pillows and a puffy comforter. It was framed on either side by matching nightstands. The room was completed with the matching dresser, and there were two doors to his right, where he assumed the closet and en-suite bathroom were located.

His gaze was pulled back to the bed. "Your bed looks so comfy." He took a running leap and threw himself onto it, only to slide straight across the bed and off onto the floor. "Oof."

"Oh my God. Are you okay?"

Brandon rushed around the bed to check on him. Nik took a moment to make sure nothing hurt. At least he had been able to use his training to roll correctly. "I'm okay. Nothing injured but my pride."

He put his hands over his face, unable to meet Brandon's gaze. "Can we just pretend that never happened?" He peeked through his fingers at Brandon. Instead of the amusement he kind of expected, he only saw concern. He lowered his hands and used them to push himself up into a sitting position and lean against the side of the bed. "Why is your bed so slippery, anyway?"

"It's a moisture-wicking comforter. I get hot, but I need to have something covering me in order to sleep."

Brandon reached out a hand and cupped Nikolai's cheek. "Are you sure you're okay?"

Nikolai nuzzled Brandon's hand, placing a kiss on his palm. "I'm fine…just embarrassed."

"Hey. What happens in this room stays in this room, as far as I'm concerned. No one else needs to know. I am sure it won't be the last embarrassing thing that happens in here."

"What makes you say that?"

It was Brandon's turn to look embarrassed, as he turned and sat down next to Nikolai on the floor and leaned against the bed. "I don't have a ton of experience. I've had hookups, but that's different. This means something and it's more than a one and done."

Nikolai stared at Brandon in shock for a moment.

"You look surprised by that."

"I am. You're perfect. I'm shocked you haven't had any relationships. I mean, at least one."

"As we discussed before, I had a plan. All I've been able to focus on up until now is that plan—until a certain blond broke my concentration, at least."

"So, clumsy does it for you, huh?" Nikolai got up and straddled Brandon's lap, wrapping his arms around his neck.

Brandon kicked up one corner of his mouth. "All of you does it for me—your brain, your body, your kisses." He put words to action and leaned in and gave Nikolai a peck on the lips.

"And you know all of you does it for me too. So, I guess we should have the other discussion too then. Top or bottom?"

"Um. I don't know. I've only had penetrative sex once. It's mainly been blow jobs and hand jobs, with occasional frottage thrown in." Brandon shrugged.

"Really?"

"Yeah. I had a kid at home. What about you? Top or bottom?"

"Well, everyone assumes I'm a bottom."

"That's not what I asked."

"I've topped exactly once and I loved it, with a guy I dated for about three months, but the guy lost his mind afterward, because he couldn't believe he let a twink like me do that to him. He broke up with me the next day."

"That is definitely his loss. I don't have an opinion or hang-ups either way, so how about we focus on just doing what feels good?"

"Sounds like a great plan to me."

Nikolai leaned forward and gave Brandon a deeper kiss, pressing his tongue in to get more of Brandon's unique flavor — one he was rapidly becoming addicted to. Who was he kidding? He was already addicted to it. With a moan, he started to circle his hips on Brandon's burgeoning hardness.

Brandon pushed him away with a gasp. "We need to get undressed. I don't want to come in my pants like a teenager. Man, you get me from zero to sixty way too fast."

Nikolai gave one more rock of his hips before standing up and backing up two steps. He unbuttoned and removed his top shirt, revealing the camisole beneath, while Brandon stared. Nikolai then offered Brandon a hand to help him up. Once they were face to face, Nik grabbed the bottom of Brandon's shirt and used the act of peeling it up and off him to feel his skin for the first time. Brandon's toned skin was gorgeous, and his brown-tinged nipples called to him. Nikolai leaned forward and took one into his mouth, giving it a gentle suck. The gasp that elicited encouraged Nik to continue, and he sucked a little harder before giving it a light nip with his teeth. That brought a full-body shudder that pleased Nikolai immensely.

Chapter Ten

Brandon looked down to find Nikolai staring back at him. His smug expression shouldn't turn him on as much as it did. He grabbed the hair at the back of Nik's head and gently pulled him away from his nipple.

"Get naked, please. I need you naked. This is gorgeous." Brandon said, running both hands down the front of the silk covering, "but I'm afraid I'm going to damage it if I try to take it off you. I want you so badly, and I need to see all of you." Nikolai gave him a look of pure want and joy that did nothing for Brandon's self-control. "Please, baby."

"You need to get naked too."

Brandon nodded repeatedly, feeling like a bobble-head doll, before reaching for his belt and making quick work of the removal of the rest of his clothes. He was so thankful that he hadn't bothered putting on socks. All the while, his gaze was transfixed on the ethereal creature in front of him — so smart, so gorgeous and all his.

Nikolai must have read the possessiveness in the way he was looking at him. "I'm all yours, *dorogoy*." Putting his hands to his hips, he pushed the skirt to his ankles and stepped out of it and the sandals he was wearing.

"Stop," Brandon choked out.

"What?" Nikolai's startled gaze met his at the sudden order.

"Holy shit, that's hot. Matching panties?"

Nikolai preened at the reaction and stood to his full height, running his hands down his chest and belly and using them to frame his hard cock where it strained against the panties' confinement. "You like?"

"I love." Brandon dropped to his knees and hesitantly ran his finger along Nik's length. The existing wet spot got larger, then he leaned forward and ran his tongue over the silk. Nik's cock spasmed and he moaned.

"Please, Brandon. I've wanted you for so long."

With one last lick, Brandon stood and pulled Nikolai into another scorching kiss. Bending his knees, he leaned down and scooped Nikolai up in a bridal carry, moving so he could lay him gently onto the bed. Reaching into the nightstand, he pulled out the new bottle of lube he had purchased and a strip of condoms.

Movement had him looking back at Nikolai and Nik did a crunch that allowed him to pull the camisole up and off. Nik's pale skin shone in the sunlight coming through the blinds. "Beautiful."

Brandon watched in fascination as a blush traveled up Nik's chest, and neck and to his face. He climbed up onto the bed and lay on his side next to Nikolai. Propping his head up on his hand, he ran a finger along Nik's chest to the edge of the remaining silk.

"You really like it?"

Brandon slowly shook his head, while looking up at Nik, letting him see his desire. "Like is too weak a word. I *love* it. It is so unbelievably sexy and knowing that I am the only one who will see what you are wearing under your clothes turns me on." Brandon drew in a shuddering breath, trying to find some control as he rocked his hard-on against Nik's hip.

Nikolai gave him a hesitant smile. "You really mean that? You don't care that I don't dress more…normal?"

"This is your normal. I accept you as you are, Nik. I want every piece of you. I'm greedy that way. I can't wait to see what else is in your wardrobe that no one else can see."

Nikolai reached out and put his hand behind Brandon's neck and pulled him into a kiss that started out gentle but quickly burned hot. Brandon moved so he was lying on top of Nikolai but braced himself on his forearms that he placed on either side of Nikolai's head so he didn't crush him. He moaned into Nikolai's mouth as he rubbed his naked cock against Nik's silk-covered one, moaning at how amazing it felt.

Nikolai gave a dirty chuckle. "Now do you see why I like the silk?"

"Oh yeah. That's amazing. Do you know what would be even better?"

"What?"

"You naked. I need you naked, babe. Like *now*." Brandon lifted himself in a push up to allow Nikolai room. Nikolai hooked his thumbs in the sides of his underwear and pushed them down as far as he could before kicking them away. Of course, it would have been easier if Brandon had been able to make himself move farther away, but that wasn't happening. With a sigh, he lowered himself again so they were skin-to-skin.

"I don't think I'm going to make it inside you this time, Nik. You feel too good."

"We've got all night. Let's take the edge off. Please...I need." He ground up into Brandon on the word 'need'. Brandon licked his hand and wrapped it around their cocks, quickly coating both of them with the plentiful pre-cum leaking out with every pull. It only took a half-dozen strokes before Nik was coming with a shout. The heat of Nikolai's cum made him follow.

Brandon gasped for air as he dropped down onto Nik, shifting a little bit so most of his weight fell to the left side of him. Brandon clunked his head onto Nik's shoulder as he continued to attempt to get his breathing under control. "That was amazing," he was able to get out after a couple minutes.

"And it's just the beginning. I can't imagine how good it's going to be when we really get comfortable with each other."

"Right?" Brandon reached out a hand to snag a couple of tissues from the box on the nightstand and swiped at their mess then half-heartedly threw the dirty tissues in the direction of the garbage can next to the bed. He'd be lucky if they made it, but that was not his concern at the moment. Rolling over onto his back, he took Nikolai with him so that Nik was able to sprawl across his chest, his head under Brandon's chin. Brandon wrapped his arms around Nik and gave him a hug, taking the opportunity to run a hand over Nik's hair that had come loose from its bun. "I love your hair. It's so gorgeous. These curls are amazing."

Nikolai chuckled against him. "Glad you approve. I've thought about chopping it off many times. It's a pain to take care of, but it's kind of my thing."

"Well, it's your hair. If you ever decide to cut it off, that's your decision."

"But you just said you love it."

"What have I been telling you? You do you. Happy Nikolai is more important to me."

Nikolai snuggled farther into Brandon's embrace. "I am so happy you decided to give us a chance."

"Me too, babe. Me too."

* * * *

Brandon woke with a start to a darkened room, his stomach rumbling in protest over not being fed. He looked down to find Nikolai staring up at him.

"I kind of feel like your stomach is getting ready to attack."

Brandon laughed. "Yeah. It's not too happy with me at the moment. How about we go get something to eat? Do you want to go out, order in or make something? What time is it anyway?"

"It's only seven thirty, but there's a thunderstorm rolling in. I've been lying here for a few minutes watching it get darker outside and listening to the thunder and your stomach."

"Yeah? Which one is angrier?"

"At the moment, your stomach." Nikolai sat up and stretched. "Which of the food options are you leaning toward?"

Brandon went to reach for Nikolai again, just as his stomach gave a vicious snarl, making Brandon wince. "I'm thinking we scrounge for a snack and order something. I don't think I have the focus to make anything decent, not that I wouldn't love to take you out and show you off," he was quick to add.

Nikolai cupped Brandon's cheek. "I know. We covered that. I would enjoy being alone with you tonight more, though."

"Me too." Brandon leaned in and took a quick kiss then scooted to the edge of the bed and stood up. He threw away the dirty tissues that did not in fact make it into the trash can, although he was pleasantly surprised that one actually had. Making his way into the bathroom, he wet two washcloths and handed one to Nik. He quickly cleaned up then went back into the bedroom to get his clothes. He pulled on his underwear and shorts as Nik searched for his own clothes and got dressed. "Leave the over-shirt off if we're not going anywhere."

"Yeah?"

"Oh yeah."

Nik was visibly pleased by his request. He leaned down and gave Nik a brief kiss before making his way to the door. "I'll meet you downstairs. I'll see what I can scrounge up for a snack. Be thinking about what you want to order."

"Okay."

Brandon opened the refrigerator and searched the contents to see what had escaped the food annihilator disguised as his brother. Grocery shopping day was usually Sunday, so he didn't have a lot of hope there would be much to offer. He was pleasantly surprised to find some cheese and grapes left. Upon closer inspection, he realized it was only because it was the sharp cheddar that Jeremy didn't like. He'd have to remember to get more.

Backing out of the refrigerator, he turned toward the counter to find Nik sitting on one of the barstools. "Hi. I didn't hear you come down."

"You were busy talking to yourself. I didn't want to interrupt."

"Ha-ha. Funny guy."

"I try. Oh, that looks good."

"At this point, I think a shoe would look good to me, but I'm excited to actually be able to offer you something. Any thoughts on what you want for dinner?" Brandon went to the cupboard to grab a knife to slice the cheese and a couple of small plates. He placed them on the counter and went to the pantry to see if he had any crackers. Spying a box, he pulled it off the shelf, only to realize it felt way too light. Glancing inside, he saw that Jeremy had put an empty box back again. With a sigh he flattened the box and placed it in recycling.

"No crackers. Sorry."

"It's all good. This is fine, since we're getting ready to order something anyway. I was thinking Italian, so that's plenty of carbs."

"Great. There's that place downtown that is really good. We can order from their website and have it delivered."

"Perfect." Nikolai reached over and grabbed one of the plates, placing some cheese and grapes on it. Leaning back in his stool, he began to nibble.

Brandon grabbed his laptop so they could order before sitting next to Nik at the breakfast bar and snagging himself some food. His stomach snarled at him as he raised the cheese to his lips.

"Feed the monster, quick." Nikolai then dissolved into giggles.

Brandon reached out and pulled Nikolai into a side hug as he used his other hand to feed himself. They were both quiet for a few minutes as they snacked. Brandon placed a kiss on the top of Nikolai's head where he was snuggled against Brandon's shoulder, before gently moving him fully into his own seat. Putting the computer in front of him, he pulled up the website for the restaurant. He closed the laptop screen a few minutes later after they'd placed their order.

"It says forty minutes. I didn't ask if you wanted something to drink."

"Water would be great. Maybe wine with dinner?"

"Okay." Brandon got up and grabbed water bottles out of the fridge, passing one over to Nikolai. "I just want to clean this mess up real quick. Meet me in the living room? I think we'll be a lot more comfortable on the couch."

"Sure." Nikolai got up and brought Brandon his plate, then went up on tiptoes to place a kiss on his cheek before making his way to the living room. Brandon watched him go for a moment, before shaking himself and focusing on what he should be doing.

It wasn't long before Brandon joined Nikolai on the couch. After sitting down next to him, he reached out and picked Nik up and placed him crosswise on his lap. Nikolai squealed and slapped his shoulder before snuggling in.

"A little warning next time. I know you said you like to cuddle, but I didn't think you meant everywhere."

Brandon thought about it for a moment. "I don't think I've had much opportunity, but I like it, especially with you."

"Aw, you say the sweetest things."

"Are you complaining?"

"About snuggling? Never. About you randomly picking me up with no warning? Yes. Although the fact that you can is a major turn-on, if I'm being completely honest."

"Which I always want you to be."

"Same goes."

"Agreed." Brandon twirled a lock of Nikolai's hair around his finger, then gently pulled so it slid loose. "Your hair is so soft."

Nikolai leaned up and pressed a kiss to Brandon's cheek. "Glad you approve. You seem to have quite the fascination with my hair."

"It's gorgeous. I keep mine super short for a reason. Otherwise, it gets out of control. It has a mind of its own. Yours always look good."

"Thank you again." Nikolai leaned up for a deeper kiss that was interrupted by the ringing doorbell.

Brandon reluctantly ended the kiss and stood with Nik in his arms, before turning and placing him back on the couch. He leaned down and placed a gentle peck on Nik's lips. "Be right back. Or better yet, do you want to meet me in the kitchen at the table?"

"Sure. I'll get drinks and silverware, too."

"Sounds good."

Dinner was a relaxed affair, with good food and better conversation.

"So," Nikolai began while twirling the last bite of his pasta on his fork and shooting shy glances at Brandon through his eyelashes. "Have you really only had penetrative sex once?"

"Yeah, but I…" Brandon stuttered to a stop.

"But you, what?"

"I didn't really enjoy it," Brandon whispered, ducking his head.

Nikolai reached out and used one finger under his chin to raise Brandon's head. "What didn't you like about it? The feeling of it?"

"No." Brandon tried to think how he was going to explain himself. "I'm in charge all the time. I have to take care of Sergei, and I have to take care of Jeremy. And I love it. I do. I just don't want to be in charge in the bedroom, but people see my size and how I am out in the world and assumes I'm some big, tough top. Does that make sense?"

Nikolai quirked an eyebrow at him. "You want someone else to take charge?"

Brandon nodded.

"Make all the decisions? Let you relax?"

Brandon nodded again.

Nikolai's eyes lit with excitement before a devilish expression crossed his face. "I am so okay with that. As I said earlier, everyone assumes I'm some submissive bottom, just waiting for a daddy. I'm so not."

The sudden feeling of relief had Brandon relaxing into his chair like his strings had been cut. "It seems we might be an even better match than we thought then?"

"Oh yeah. Now let's clean up this mess, because I know it will drive you crazy otherwise, then let's head back to the bedroom. We have some exploring to do."

They stood and quickly cleaned up the mess before Nikolai grabbed Brandon's hand and pulled him up the stairs.

Chapter Eleven

Nikolai felt like Christmas and his birthday had come all at once. His dream man was willing to give up control to him in the bedroom, something no one else had ever wanted. He hadn't told Brandon how horrible his ex had been to him when he'd broken up with him the next day.

His parting words had stuck with Nik for a long time. *"I was dating you because you look pretty on my arm, but you always think you're so smart, because you are getting your doctorate. I don't need a power bottom or someone who thinks they can top me. I only did it yesterday because of all your whining. So not attractive."* Like he wasn't allowed to be anything other than an accessory.

Nikolai shook himself and focused on the here and now. He had a sexy as fuck man to explore. That required all his attention. Nikolai made it to the bedroom without incident and pulled Brandon around in front of him a few feet from the bed. "Strip, Whitaker."

Nikolai watched in fascination as a shudder went through Brandon at the command before he raised his hands and stripped off his shirt. Nikolai walked in a slow circle around Brandon, running his fingers over different parts of his torso as he did so. He stopped behind Brandon to nip at his ear. He was pleased at the gasp that elicited. Brandon struggled to open the button on his shorts, finally getting them undone. Nikolai pushed the shorts off Brandon's hips to pool around his feet on the floor.

Nik continued his slow walk around Brandon until he was once again facing him. He ran a finger up Brandon's already-leaking cock and covered his finger in the pre-cum at the head. He made eye contact with Brandon to make sure he was watching as he raised his hand to his lips and ran his tongue over his finger to clean it off. "So tasty. I'm a lucky man to have such a delicious boyfriend. I foresee many pleasurable hours sucking you off in our future."

"As long as" — Brandon stopped to clear his throat — "I can return the favor."

"Oh yes, that is the plan. Get up on the bed, Brandon. On your back." Nikolai waited until Brandon complied. "Watch me."

Nikolai pushed his skort down to the floor, leaving himself in his panties and camisole. He was gratified to hear Brandon start to pant. Brandon reached for his cock. "Uh-uh. That's mine. Hands up and grab the headboard."

Brandon shot his hands up, but there was no way he could grab the sleigh bed headboard, as it was all one piece. "Hm-m. We may have to invest in some straps, *dorogoy*. Just keep your hands up above your head for now. I didn't really get a chance to explore earlier."

Brandon groaned loudly, causing Nikolai to grin. "Now I know you love this outfit, but I really think naked exploration would be better. Don't you?"

Brandon nodded. "Oh yes. Please."

Nikolai stripped off his remaining clothing, making sure to do a slow reveal—first his top then his panties, before he went to the bed and knee-walked until he was straddling Brandon's hips. He didn't lower down, though. He just kneeled there, looking at him.

"Nikolai, please touch me. I need you to touch me."

Nikolai ran both hands up Brandon's chest, giving both nipples a tweak on his way by. "Patience. You'll get what you need. I'm assuming you didn't do any prep for bottoming today?"

Brandon looked shocked then embarrassed. "No. I assumed you would want me to top."

"Well, we'll have to take care of that later. For now, let me play with my new toy." Nik leaned forward making sure to rub their chests together as he reached to place a kiss on Brandon's lips. Then Nik lay kisses in a trail across Brandon's jaw before sucking his left earlobe into his mouth.

"Hot spot," he breathed against Brandon's ear, as Brandon gave a full body shudder beneath him.

"I didn't know," Brandon gasped out.

"Hm-m. Lucky me to be the one to find it.

"I think it's actually lucky me."

Nik licked his way down Brandon's neck and down over his collarbone to his nipple. Brandon arched into Nikolai's mouth. Nikolai came off the left one with a pop and made his way to the right one, where he gave it the same treatment.

"Please, Nik. I need more."

"Yeah. I think we need to move this show along. I want you too much, even after earlier. One day, maybe I'll be able to take my time and appreciate you like I want to."

Brandon crunched up to give Nikolai a brief peck then laid back on the bed. "I'll look forward to it."

Nik leaned forward and gave Brandon another kiss, letting this one build in voracity until they were both gasping and writhing together. Nikolai shoved himself up and back. "No. I need you inside me this time. Hold still. Now where are the condoms and lube?"

Brandon waved a hand at where he had set everything earlier. Nikolai snagged them and rolled a condom down Brandon's long, thick length. Opening the lube, he squirted some onto his fingers and reached behind himself to open himself up—only having the patience to get two fingers in before he was squirting more lube into his hand to apply to Brandon. Kneeling up again, he used one hand to position Brandon at his hole. "Don't you dare move, Brandon. This is my show."

Nikolai watched as Brandon's eyes dilated even farther as he started to lower himself. He made himself go slow, keeping eye contact with Brandon the entire time. He allowed himself a moment to enjoy how full he was when he finally reached the bottom, wiggling a little bit to seat himself more solidly.

"Can I touch you now? I need to touch you."

"Not yet," Nik gasped as he raised himself equally slowly until he'd almost pulled off, and then dropping back down with only a slight hesitation. He kept the pace tortoise slow until Brandon pressed up in counterpoint on the next dropdown, rubbing against his prostate just right. "Naughty boy."

"Please. Let me touch you."

Nikolai noted the desperation in Brandon's voice with satisfaction. "Yes."

He barely got the word out and he felt Brandon's hands on his hips, using his grip to drive up into Nikolai, while pulling him down at the same time. Nikolai gasped at a particularly well-placed hit to his prostate. Brandon adjusted and made an effort to hit that spot obviously, because the next three strokes were to the exact same location.

Nikolai reached a shaking hand for his cock and started pulling on it in time with their bodies coming together. It didn't take long until he felt the familiar tingle signaling the end was near. "Come with me, Brandon. Come. Right. *Now*!"

With a shout, Brandon started coming. Nikolai could feel the pulses in his channel as he made sure to paint Brandon's chest with his own release. He sagged forward, and Brandon wrapped his arms around him, pulling him tighter into the squishy mess between them.

Brandon started laughing. Nikolai couldn't help but stare as he saw Brandon's happiness. "What's so funny?"

"I finally see what all the hype about sex is about. That was amazing. I can't wait to see how it feels when you're inside me."

Nikolai leaned up and gave Brandon another soft kiss. "Glad to be the one to show you."

"I think, if I'm being honest, that you are probably the only one who could." Brandon ran a hand from the back of Nikolai's head, down to his ass. "We should probably get cleaned up," he said with a yawn.

"Yeah." Nikolai pulled himself off Brandon and rolled to the side to lay on his back. He turned to look at Brandon to find him already staring at him. "What?"

"I love you. I know it's quick, since we just started this, but I love you."

Nikolai raised a hand to Brandon's cheek. "I love you too. I have for a while, even more now, though, since I'm getting to see all of you."

Brandon leaned over and kissed Nikolai. "Shower with me?"

"I'd love to." Nikolai stood up and groaned.

Brandon was suddenly by his side. "What's the matter?"

"Haven't done that in a while, and you're not a small man, Brandon. Don't worry. It's a good sore, though."

"You sure?"

"Yep. You'll know the feeling soon enough." Nikolai stopped to yawn. "Just not today. Man, I'm beat."

Brandon yawned as well. "Don't do that. Now you've got me yawning. Let's get in the shower and get clean, since we both obviously need some sleep."

Nikolai trudged behind Brandon to the bathroom, struggling to keep his eyes open. He stopped to use the toilet before joining Brandon in the shower. Stepping into Brandon's space, he wrapped his arms around him from behind and just enjoyed the closeness for a moment. He tightened his arms in a hug before reaching for the soap to start running it over Brandon's chest in lazy circles from behind.

"Here... Give me that. At this rate we're never going to get out of here." Nikolai watched in bemusement as Brandon washed up and rinsed with clinical precision before stepping aside and letting Nikolai into the water stream. When Nikolai reached for the soap, Brandon held it out of reach. "Let me take care of you." Brandon squirted some shampoo into his hand and massaged it into Nikolai's hair. The gentle motion almost lulled Nikolai to sleep. When prompted, he tilted his head back and rinsed the soap out. Brandon then washed Nikolai's body with the same gentle attention. Before he knew it, he was standing on the bathmat, being tenderly dried by his lover.

"Hi," he mumbled when Brandon's face appeared in front of his.

He felt the puffs of air from Brandon's chuckle on his lips. "You have crashed. Come on. Let's get in bed."

Nikolai let himself be led to the bedroom and tucked into bed. He rolled toward Brandon when he climbed in the other side, draping himself over Brandon's chest and entwining their legs together. "I was so worried that we were one, never going to get together, and two, that if we did get together, we would be horrible in bed. I'm so happy I worried for nothing."

"We are very good together, aren't we?" Brandon sounded very smug as he asked the question.

"We are. So happy."

Nikolai let himself float off to sleep to the sound of Brandon's. "Me too."

Chapter Twelve

Brandon was standing at the stove making bacon when steps sounded behind him. A barely awake Nikolai was rubbing at his right eye while staring at him. "Good morning, babe. Breakfast is almost ready. Coffee is over there." Turning back to the bacon, he heard Nikolai shuffling toward the Keurig.

"Cups?"

"In the cupboard above the coffee maker. Pods and sugar are right there next to it. We mainly just have the plain dark-roast kind, not any of the flavors. Creamer is in the refrigerator. Not sure how you take it."

"Just a little sugar. Anything else is too much work first thing. I save the complicated drinks for Starbucks."

"Sounds reasonable to me."

"You don't drink coffee. Why do you have a coffee maker?"

Brandon startled and looked over at Nikolai. "How did you know I don't drink coffee?"

Nikolai waved at himself. "Stalker, remember? I noticed you never drink coffee. Usually water or a soda, if you have anything."

"I don't like the taste of it. Smell? Yes. Taste? No. Jeremy has a mildish case of ADHD—not enough to warrant meds, but bad enough to be noticeable some days. We try to watch what he eats, but his doctor recommended a cup of coffee in the morning. The caffeine is a stimulant like Ritalin. One cup in the morning usually helps him focus." Brandon gave a half-shrug. "It's a pretty simple way to manage it, hence the coffee maker."

"Makes sense. Glad you have it, to be honest."

"Well, if you're going to be spending more nights here—and I hope you will—you'll have to tell me what kind you like so we can get it for you."

"While that's very sweet, what you have works. What do you need me to do?"

"Sit at the counter, drink your coffee and talk to me. As I said, everything is almost ready."

"All right."

Brandon plated the food and turned toward the counter to find Nikolai working on the copy of the sudoku puzzle that had been laying there. Glancing down, he realized that Nikolai had almost completed the puzzle in the few minutes that he had been finishing cooking breakfast. He could only stare in amazement. Nikolai obviously feeling his stare, looked up at him.

"What?"

"You've almost finished the puzzle."

"And?"

"In ink."

"And? It's what was here to write with."

"Do you see how many copies are there? Jeremy and I pick a puzzle out of the sudoku book and make copies that we use as we try to fill them out. We have been working on this one for three weeks." Shaking his head, he put the plates down on the counter.

"Um. Sorry?"

"Nothing to be sorry for," he said as he sat down in his seat. "I'm just amazed by you is all." He watched as a suddenly shy Nikolai ducked his head in obvious embarrassment.

"Numbers make sense to me...always have." Nikolai glanced up at him. After picking up his fork, he took a bite of the food. "Thank you for making breakfast, by the way."

"No problem. It's one of the few meals I can usually manage to not screw up."

"Well, it's good." He looked deep in thought for a moment. "Anyway, back to what I was saying. I've always loved the logic of numbers. You can line them up and they behave. Their logic never changes."

"Even when you add a letter?"

"Especially when you add a letter. The letter is saying 'Hello there. I'm really a number. Tell me what number I am'."

Brandon snorted out a laugh. "Too funny. Maybe you can give Jeremy and me some tips about figuring these out. I mean, I can do spreadsheets and such, but for some reason, these do my head in."

"I'd be happy to show you guys some tricks. They're fun."

"You're weird."

Nikolai waggled his head side to side. "Eh. I resemble that remark. I own it."

Brandon could only chuckle at the response. "Speaking of fun, what do you want to do today? We still have several hours before we have to be at Mama H's." A loud boom of thunder made them both jump. "Let me rephrase. What do you want to do *inside*? Hope this clears up before the barbecue tonight."

"It's only supposed to rain this morning. How about I introduce you to the original *Star Trek*, while our food digests?"

"And after that?"

Nikolai shot him a wicked grin and an eyebrow waggle. "Then we can see if I missed any of your hotspots."

"I'm in."

"Thought you might be."

* * * *

Walking around the Hamilton house to the backyard as per instructions hours later, Brandon had to focus to make sure he was walking in a straight line.

"You okay there?" Brandon could just see Nikolai's cocky expression from the corner of his eye, and Nikolai truly had a strut going on. "There's no need to be smug. You know you rocked my world."

Nikolai pulled Brandon into a brief hug and placed a kiss on his cheek, whispering in his ear. "And I look forward to doing it again."

"Me too," Brandon whispered, before giving Nikolai a not-so-chaste kiss back.

"Ew. Germs." The chorus of teen boy voices made them startle apart.

Nikolai wrapped his arms around Brandon's waist. "Jealous?"

Jessie raised his hand. "I am."

"What?" Jeremy's screech was comical.

"Sorry, Jeremy. Your brother is hot."

"Bones! Do you hear this? I've been betrayed. You're my best friend now."

"Sorry, Jeremy, but empirically speaking, your brother *is* hot. I'm not gay, but even I can see that."

"What about me?" Nikolai asked with an obviously fake whine.

Sasha waved him off. "You know you're gorgeous, cuz. Stop fishing for compliments."

"Yeah," Brandon whispered to him, "stop fishing for compliments." With another chuckle he stepped away from Nikolai and snagged his hand so they could continue walking around the house. "Hey, Sasha, Nikolai made me watch several episodes of the original *Star Trek* this morning. I get the Bones reference now."

"He says several. He means two. I made him watch *two* episodes," Nikolai told them.

"Was that all? Huh. Felt like more," Brandon replied.

Sasha looked at him with wide eyes. "Are you saying you didn't like it, Brandon?"

Brandon stage-whispered back. "I kind of did, but don't tell anyone, okay? It will be our little secret."

Sasha laughed and mimed zipping his lips closed.

"Good boy. Now, how did auditions go? Jeremy wouldn't tell me anything until he could see me face-to-face."

Jeremy was almost skipping as he walked beside Brandon. "It was amazing, Brandon. First, we had to do our prepared piece. Then they handed us a sheet of paper, and we had to memorize as much as we could in two minutes. That was so fun."

"Fun is not how I would describe it," Sasha moaned. "That was hard."

Jeremy laughed, then shrugged. "Well, it helps I have a great memory. Your singing audition went fantastic, though. Yours and Jessie's both."

"You did okay, too. You haven't had singing lessons like me and Bones. You would probably be better than us if you did."

"You think?"

Sasha and Jessie both nodded. "You should have seen him, Brandon. He completely lit up on stage. He's a natural."

"Okaaaayyy. Does that mean he got a part? And what about the two of you?"

All three of the boys laughed. Jessie was the one to answer, though. "Yeah, we all got parts. Sasha and I both got leads."

"And I get to be in the chorus." Jeremy bounced around until he was in front of Brandon, walking backward.

"And you are excited about being in the chorus?"

"Yep. I get to hang with Bones and Jessie, but I don't have to be at every rehearsal. I also get to learn more about the theater stuff they love so much."

"Plus, he gets to be with Julia in the chorus," Sasha added dryly.

"Ah. Now the truth comes out. Is Julia the current love interest?"

Jeremy's 'no' was drowned out by Sasha and Jessie's 'yes' while Jeremy flushed an interesting shade of pink. Luckily for Jeremy, they arrived at the backyard.

"Oh, look. Your mom brought more food out, Bones. Let's go see what's there," Jeremy said then darted away. The other two followed him, mocking him the entire time.

Nikolai and Brandon shared a look, before bursting into laughter.

"Now I understand Jeremy's sudden interest in theater," Brandon said.

Nikolai pulled on Brandon's hand, getting him moving again. "Yep. Let's go get some food before the piranhas eat it all."

"Good plan."

Chapter Thirteen

Nikolai was so busy daydreaming about his sexy boyfriend and the last couple of months of dating that he really wasn't seeing anything on the computer screen in front of him. A throat clearing behind him made him jump and look toward Kirk's office door.

"Oh hey, Kirk. What's up?"

"Wondering where your head's at today. I've been standing here five minutes, and you haven't moved at all."

"Sorry. I'm having a focus issue."

"I see that. Can I ask why? Everything going okay with you and Brandon?"

Nikolai sighed heavily. "Everything's going great with me and Brandon."

"Why do you make it sound like that's a bad thing?"

"It's not." Nikolai spun to face Kirk, and Nikolai slumped in his chair when he saw Kirk's disbelieving expression. "I'm just not used to relationships going well. I don't quite know how to act. I mean it's been almost two months and I'm falling for him a little more every day. We had a few hiccups in the beginning, but we've really worked on communication and…" Nikolai ran out of steam. "It's going to gut me once he realizes how annoying I am and dumps me."

"You really think that's going to happen? That man worships you."

"That man avoided me for years because he didn't want a relationship."

"Which should tell you that he's all in now. He thought about it, got to know you and decided you were worth changing his plans for. You know that man is all about his plans. You also know that man adores every neurotic, brilliant bit of you."

"I know that intellectually. I'm just waiting for the other shoe to drop."

"Well, stop it! Enjoy what you have instead of borrowing trouble."

"You're right."

"What's on your agenda for the holiday weekend?"

"It's Animazement weekend in downtown Raleigh. Sasha and Jessie are staying over tonight so we can all go to the con together tomorrow. Since we don't know how late it will be when we finish, the boys are staying over again on Saturday and will go home Sunday morning. No idea what the rest of the weekend plans are, but Animazement is always a good time."

"Yeah? Who are you going as?"

Nikolai shifted in his seat and couldn't make eye contact. "Um. It's between two costumes. Either Legolas from *Lord of the Rings*…" Nikolai's voice trailed off.

"Or?"

"Or Gamora from *Guardians of the Galaxy*."

Kirk blinked at Nikolai for a moment, then a grin creased his face. "You would so rock the Gamora costume."

Nikolai let out the breath he'd been holding, as he distantly heard the door chime behind him. "You don't think it would embarrass Jeremy?"

"Have Jeremy or any of his friends cared about any of your other clothing choices?"

"Well, no, but I've tried to tone it down when I'm around them."

"Why the hell would you do that?"

Nikolai spun around to face the door when Brandon asked the question. Jeremy was standing right behind him, peeking at Nikolai over Brandon's shoulder.

"Yeah, dude. Why would you do that? I don't care what you wear."

"I don't want to embarrass you."

"Be you, dude. Wear what you want. Jessie's going as Nurse Chapel from the original *Star Trek*. He wanted me to ask if you could do his makeup. I think he's going to look amazing. Bones is going as, well…Bones, and I'm going as Spock. It's going to be so much fun."

Brandon spoke to Kirk. "Mind if we steal him for lunch, Kirk?"

"Not at all. In fact, it's really quiet today. Why don't you go ahead and leave for the day?"

"Are you sure?"

"Yep. Get out of here. Enjoy your weekend. I'll see you Tuesday."

"Thanks, Bossman."

Kirk waved him away. Nikolai quickly shut down the spreadsheets he was working on, leaving the garage software programs running. He grabbed his things before turning to look at Brandon and Jeremy again. He flinched a little when he found Brandon giving him a hard stare with his arms crossed.

"Hey, Jeremy," Kirk interrupted the stare down. "Why don't you come hang with me while your brother helps Nikolai get his things from upstairs?"

"You mean while Nikolai and Brandon have a discussion." Jeremy put air quotes around the word 'discussion', making Kirk laugh.

"Yep. We don't want your young innocent ears to be offended. I have a feeling it could get loud."

"Sure." Jeremy moved around Brandon and walked into Kirk's office, talking Kirk's ear off the entire way about all the things he was planning to do with his friends over the weekend.

Nikolai waved a hand in the direction of the door that led upstairs to his apartment from the garage. "Let's head upstairs. You can yell at me there."

Brandon gave an exasperated sigh. "I'm not going to yell at you, Nikolai. I'm not a yeller."

"I almost wish you were. This disappointed look you're wearing is brutal."

Brandon shook his head. "Get upstairs. Everyone doesn't need to hear our discussion."

As soon as they were through the door, Brandon grabbed his arm, spun him around and pressed his back against the door. Brandon leaned into him, supporting his upper body with his forearms on either side of Nikolai's head.

"What's going on in that brain of yours? I thought we'd already discussed this. Be you. Jeremy adores you as you. He doesn't care. His friends don't care. If someone cares, they aren't in our circle of friends. Now, what's really got you spooked?"

"I don't want you to get sick of me. Everyone says I'm really annoying. I don't have a lot of friends. Even my own parents can't stand me."

"Sergei adores you."

Nikolai scoffed. "Sergei is an asshole."

"True, but he adores you and would do anything for you, as would any of the rest of his immediate family. The guys here at the garage consider you a friend. They invite you to do things with them. Sensei and the other instructors at the dojo have all pulled me aside and threatened me if I hurt you in any way."

Nikolai felt his eyes get big. "They did not."

Brandon nodded sharply. "They did. They all adore you and are happy that we're together. You need to be happy too. Are you happy with me, Nik?"

Nikolai bobbed his head up and down. "I'm so happy. I love you so much, and I don't want to lose you."

Brandon leaned his head down and kissed Nikolai breathless. "I told you. I'm not going anywhere. You need to relax. We're going to fight. We're two very different people. We aren't always going to agree but know that I love you and will fight *for* you way more than I will ever fight against you."

Nikolai's eyes filled with tears and he tried to blink them away. Brandon lifted a hand and gently used his thumb to wipe away one that had escaped, despite his best efforts. Brandon stole another kiss before stepping away.

"Now. Go get your things. We have a very full weekend to prepare for."

"What do you have going on?"

"I'm going to the convention with you, of course. I need to make sure no one tries to steal you away from me, especially if you are going to be wearing something sexy."

Nik snorted a laugh. "You think I'm sexy no matter what I wear."

"That's true. Get your stuff."

Nik went to his bedroom and grabbed his garment bag containing his two costume options, the additional bag for his shoe choices and the duffle bag with clothes for the rest of the weekend. Regular classes at the dojo had finished for the year, and it was on a break for a month to allow kids to finish up the school year and all the end-of-school-year events without conflict. Summer classes would start late June, but Nikolai was taking a break to focus on work, the center and his relationship.

He returned to the front door, and Brandon took the garment bag as well as the shoe bag, leaving Nik to carry his duffle. Nik went up on his toes and gave Brandon a kiss on the cheek as he passed him. "Thank you."

"For what?"

"Being you. Loving me. Take your pick."

"You never have to thank me for loving you. It's my pleasure."

"Gag. Must you two be so mushy all the time."

"Yep. It's in the parental by-laws. Must embarrass and or disgust the teenager at least one time per day."

Kirk chuckled. "Section six, subsection twelve, right, Brandon?"

"Ha-ha. You guys are not as funny as you think you are. We ready to go now?"

"Yep. What time are the guys coming over?"

"They'll be to our house at six. Dinner and sleepover, then to the con first thing tomorrow."

Nik threw an arm across Jeremy's shoulders and started steering him toward the door. "Sounds good. I plan on just going Saturday morning this year and leave after lunch—let you young things carry the torch."

"Plus, it means you and Brandon get some alone time Saturday afternoon. You're not fooling me."

"That may have factored into the decision as well." Nikolai couldn't hide his grin.

"Make sure you guys take lots of pictures. We're going up to my in-laws' lake house, so we won't be around," Kirk said.

"Will do. Have a great weekend, Boss."

Kirk rolled his eyes at Nikolai. "Get out of here."

The three of them loaded into the car. "What are you doing out of school, anyway?"

"Teacher workday."

"Ah. Okay. What are you guys feeling for lunch?"

"Well, since you don't have to go right back, why don't we head home and cook something? I know Jeremy's going to be eating a lot of junk food all weekend, starting with pizza tonight. Might not be a bad idea to get something somewhat healthy into him for lunch."

"Sounds good. Maybe we can grill something? It's a perfect day for it."

Jeremy chimed in from the back seat. "I'll eat anything. I'm starving."

"There's a shocker. You're always starving, brother of mine."

"Yep. Feed me."

Brandon's phone began to ring right after he pulled into the garage and put the car in park. Brandon made a weird face that Nikolai couldn't decipher then answered the phone.

"Whitaker. What can I do for you, Mrs. Johnson?"

A squeak from the backseat made Nikolai turn to look at Jeremy, to find him staring in horror at Brandon. Nikolai signaled for Jeremy to step out of the car. "Who's Mrs. Johnson?"

"She was our CPS caseworker, but we haven't heard from her in like three years. I have no idea why she is calling. I didn't do anything."

Nikolai stopped and placed both his hands on Jeremy's shoulders. "Take a deep breath. I'm sure it's nothing you did. Brandon will handle it, whatever it is. Now, breathe with me. In." Deep inhale. "Out." Long exhale. "Okay. In through your nose. Out through your mouth. That's good."

Brandon opened his car door and they both spun to look at him. He was pale and shaking. "What's wrong?" Nikolai rushed to get around the car to him, pulling him into his arms as soon as he was close enough.

"Our mom is in the hospital with stage four breast cancer. She wants to see us." Brandon stopped to swallow hard.

Jeremy exploded. "Oh hell no. I don't want to see her."

"They don't think she's going to live too much longer, Jer." Brandon clutched Nikolai harder, before making direct eye contact with Jeremy. "There's more."

"What?"

"We have a sister. She's three, almost four, I guess. Mom has named me guardian. They need me to come get her if I want her."

Jeremy collapsed to sit on the step leading into the house. "We have a *sister*?"

"Yep. Listen... Why don't we all head into the house and talk about it."

Nikolai pulled back to look at Brandon. "Do you want me to leave?"

"No! This involves you too. I know you didn't sign up for..."

Nikolai placed his hand on Brandon's cheek, making him look at him. "Don't you dare finish that sentence. I signed up to be with you, no matter where that takes us. We're trying to be family, right?"

"Yeah."

"And we already talked about children in the future."

"Yeah, but that was in the future...not now."

"Well, this is the path fate decided for us. Let's go in like you said and all talk it through."

Nikolai took Brandon's hand and led him into the house, following a very quiet and contained Jeremy. Jeremy threw himself onto the couch with a huff. Nikolai sat next to the teen while Brandon sat on the coffee table in front of them. Jeremy crossed his arms and tapped his foot for a few moments before blurting out his thoughts. "I still don't want to see Mom, but I think having a little sister would be cool."

"Well, if I took her, I would want to adopt her."

"Awesome. Then I'll have a brother-dad and a sister two ways."

Nikolai stared at Jeremy for a moment before bursting into laughter. "Oh, Jeremy, I adore you."

"Yeah, well, you make my brother happy, so I adore you too."

"This will be a big change for all of us. Three years old is not fifteen." Brandon looked at Nikolai and Jeremy intently, obviously trying to gauge their reactions.

"Eh. We'll adapt. It's what we do. We can't let her go to someone else. She's ours." Jeremy's vehemence surprised Nikolai.

"My only question is, will it be a problem for the adoption process if we're dating?"

"I wouldn't think so, since my mother is leaving guardianship to me rather than me suing her for custody. The caseworker, Mrs. Robinson, knows I'm gay."

"She does?"

"Yep. It came up in the custody hearing for Jeremy. I can ask her when we meet her at the hospital if you're worried about it, though."

"It would make me feel better if everything is out in the open."

"Then that's what we'll do." Brandon leaned forward and took Nikolai's hand in his. "But know this. I'm not giving you up, so if that's what you're thinking, forget it. If we have to, we'll pull Sergei into this. Okay?"

"Okay," Nikolai answered, leaning forward to place a kiss on Brandon's lips. "We're all in this together."

"Now, we should probably get going. What time are the guys getting here, Jeremy?"

"Six o'clock. Can they still come over?"

"I don't see why not. Life goes on. Are you sure you don't want to come see Mom? From what Mrs. Robinson said, this may be our last chance." Brandon held up his hand before Jeremy could speak. "No judgment. Just think about it for a minute. Mom had scheduled a meeting with Mrs. Robinson, and when she got there Mrs. Robinson found her collapsed on the floor. Mrs. Robinson called an ambulance then took our sister with her, so our sister is in the hospital room with Mom and Mrs. Robinson, waiting for us."

Jeremy blew out a long breath. "Yeah. Let's go. We should meet her as a family."

"That's my boy."

"I *am*, too. You know that right? You've always done a great job taking care of me, even before you got custody."

Brandon leaned forward and grabbed Jeremy by the back of the neck, pulling him in so they were leaning forehead to forehead. "I've tried my best."

"And we'll all do the same with..." Jeremy's nose scrunched in confusion. "What's her name?"

Brandon laughed. "You know, Mrs. Robinson told me, but I don't remember. Let's go find out."

"Okay. Can we grab something to eat on the way?"

"Yeah. That sounds like a plan."

Chapter Fourteen

Brandon took a bracing breath and tried to force a smile as he entered the hospital room. He was gripping Nikolai's hand so hard that he was sure it wasn't comfortable, but he couldn't seem to force himself to let go. He looked back to make sure Jeremy was still with them, before turning his attention to the occupants of the room. A gasp escaped him when he saw his mother. She was hooked up to multiple machines, with an oxygen cannula in her nose, and was a shadow of her former self. She had a colorful scarf on her head, but that was the only color to be found.

A noise had him looking to his left to find a little girl with dark, kinky curls coming out of the bathroom. Mrs. Robinson was following behind her.

"Mrs. Robinson," Brandon greeted.

"Oh, Brandon, you made it, and Jeremy, I almost didn't recognize you. You've grown so much since the last time I saw you."

"Yes, ma'am. Brandon takes good care of me." Jeremy's defensive tone had Brandon reaching out and squeezing his shoulder.

"It's all good, Jer. You're mine. Okay?"

Jeremy's shoulders relaxed. "Yeah. Sorry. Reflex."

"I know...but breathe." He waited until Jeremy sucked in a shaky breath, before turning his attention back to Mrs. Robinson and the little girl staring up at him. "Hi, sweetie." Brandon moved forward, releasing Nikolai and Jeremy and getting down on one knee in front of her. "What's your name?"

"I'm Casey. I'm three." She held up three fingers as she answered.

"Nice to meet you, Casey. Do you know who I am?"

The little girl nodded rapidly, her curls flying all over. "You're my brother Brandon and you're going to be my new daddy and take care of me, because Mommy is sick."

"That's right."

"And I'm your brother Jeremy." Jeremy joined him on the floor in front of the little girl.

"Hi, Jer-my."

"Can I pick you up? There's someone else I'd like you to meet."

Casey threw herself into Brandon's arms and hugged him tightly around the neck. Brandon stood and turned toward Nikolai to find him recording the meeting on his phone. He gave Brandon a crooked grin.

"For posterity."

Brandon grinned back. "Mrs. Robinson. Casey, this is my boyfriend, Nikolai."

"It's a pleasure to meet you, Nikolai." Mrs. Robinson bustled forward and shook Nikolai's hand.

"It's not going to be a problem is it, ma'am?"

"Oh no. Not a problem at all. I'm assuming it's serious, since you came with them?"

"Yes, ma'am."

"Good. Brandon deserves serious."

"Yes, he does."

Casey was staring at the adults while they talked. Nikolai stepped forward and ran his hand over her curls. "Hi, Casey. I'm very happy to meet you."

"You're pretty. Are you an angel?"

"No. I'm definitely not an angel. I'm just Nikolai — or you can call me Nik, okay?"

Casey nodded and reached her arms out for Nikolai. She then laid her head on Nikolai's shoulder with a shuddering sigh, put her thumb in her mouth and appeared to fall asleep. Brandon could only blink at how quickly she was out. He looked at Mrs. Robinson in shock.

"She's exhausted. She's been worried no one was going to come. She probably won't sleep long, though."

"What about her father? Doesn't he want her?"

"Your mother doesn't know who that is. It seems she went out to cheer herself up on the one-year anniversary of losing custody of your brother and had a one-night stand. She was unable to locate him again." Mrs. Robinson shrugged. "As I said, she has named you guardian and wants you to adopt her outright. All the paperwork is in order, just waiting on signatures. We won't have to go through the whole process that you did with Jeremy."

"Has she been cared for?"

"Yes. Your mother got clean when she found out she was pregnant and, by all accounts, has stayed clean."

"I did my best," a weak voice said from the bed.

"Mom!"

"Oh, you both look so good." Their mom raised her hands to her mouth and had tears in her eyes.

Jeremy and Brandon went to stand on either side of her bed. Brandon distantly noted that Mrs. Robinson and Nikolai took Casey out of the room to allow them privacy.

"Hi, boys."

"Hi, Mom," Jeremy whispered. "I'm sorry you're sick."

"I know you are, baby. You were always such a gentle soul. I'm sorry I couldn't get myself together to be the mother you deserved. I hear from Mrs. Robinson that Brandon is doing a great job with you, though."

"He's a great dad slash brother. I'm happy with him." Jeremy stared at her for a moment longer before leaning down and kissing her cheek. "I know you probably won't get better, but we're doing good. You don't have to worry about us." Jeremy then stepped back from the bed and waved his hand in the direction of the door. "I'm just going to go be with Casey and Nik. I don't really have anything else to say." He stopped at the door and turned back to whisper, "Bye, Mom. I love you."

"Bye, baby. I love you, too."

She turned to Brandon and stared at him for a long moment, the exhaustion and pain very evident. "I'm so proud of you. You've become the man your father would have wanted you to be. I know I made you be a grown-up way sooner than you should have had to, and that's on me." Her eyes filled with tears. "Your father would be so disappointed."

Brandon looked at her, so frail and sick in her hospital bed, not sure how he felt about that statement. "I don't know what you want me to say. Addiction is an illness, but you let yourself wallow in it. It didn't feel like you even tried. I mean…I'm glad that you've been able to pull it together for Casey. That's a very good thing. She seems happy and healthy, but it doesn't mean I'm not still angry."

"I know." She closed her eyes for a moment before blinking them back open. "I was trying to get better so I could contact you. I worked so hard, but then I found out about the cancer. I was hoping I could beat this, and we could be a family again."

"Why didn't you contact us before it got to this stage? Why wait until the last minute? You're not giving any of us time to adjust, and now you want me to raise another of your children?"

"It's a lot to ask, but I wouldn't trust her with anyone else. As far as why I waited, it really hasn't been that long. I was already stage three when they found it. I put off having a mammogram and justified it by saying I didn't have time. I should have contacted you right away. I've reacted badly to the chemo. My alcoholism and former drug use already caused a weakness in my heart and it's not handling the treatments. It was another mistake, not to contact you sooner. I'm sorry." She broke off with a sob.

Brandon grabbed a tissue from the rolling table that held her water glass and handed it to her. Lowering the side bar, he gently sat on the bed and pulled her into his arms, holding and rocking her until she finally quieted. "I know you're sorry, Mom. I know, but it will take me a while to get my head around everything." Brandon took a moment to organize his thoughts. He glanced over his shoulder through the open doorway to see Nik rocking the still sleeping Casey in his arms in the hallway just outside the door, while Jeremy was having an animated conversation with Mrs. Robinson. His heart lurched with love for Nik, Jeremy and Casey. Yes, he already loved her, and he looked forward to learning who she was and who she would be. Turning back to his mother, he kissed her on the top of the head before gently moving her back to rest on the bed. "I will take Casey and raise her as my own. Nik, Jeremy and I will take great care of her."

"So, Nik? Is it serious?"

"Yes…very." Brandon looked over his shoulder again and couldn't help his besotted smile. Casey suddenly lifted her head and looked around wildly. When she saw Brandon looking at her, she started waving to him. "Oh Lord. She's another dynamo like Jeremy, isn't she?"

Turning back, his mother quirked a tired grin at him. "Yep. The child never stops moving or talking. Even when she was a baby, she would hum or babble all the time."

Brandon looked at her seriously. "I'll look forward to hearing it all."

His mom raised a shaking hand to his cheek and patted it gently, before letting it fall to the bed. "I know you will. I've signed all the papers already. Mrs. Robinson has the key to our apartment, so you can get all Casey's things and the paperwork for you to sign. I'm afraid there isn't much left. Treatment has been expensive, and she seems to outgrow her clothes so fast." The last was spoken in barely a whisper that Brandon had to lean forward to hear.

"It's all good, Mama. We'll get her things."

"Thank you, Brandon. Know that I love you all." She was barely audible now.

"I know, Mama. I know you love us, and you just couldn't figure out how to make it all work without Dad. I love you too."

"I hope one day you will think of me positively...all of you."

"I'll tell them about you, about how you were with Dad. That was your best you."

"It really was." Her eyes closed and the last of the tension left her body. He heard her saying, "I hope he's waiting for me." He jumped when an alarm suddenly started going off and he heard running feet. A nurse ushered Brandon away from the bed and out into the hall with everyone else. He watched in horror as he realized that her heart had stopped beating right before the door to the room closed. He turned around to look at his family, just in time to catch Jeremy as he threw himself at him.

"Is she dead?"

Brandon ran his hand up and down Jeremy's back. "I don't know yet. We'll have to wait for the doctor to come out."

"I-I didn't want her to die."

"I know, buddy. I know. You still have me, though. I'm not going anywhere."

Jeremy slumped into Brandon's arms. "I have you and Nik and Casey and all of our friends. We're very lucky, aren't we?"

"We really are." Brandon looked over Jeremy's shoulder to find Nikolai standing and holding a crying Casey, trying to soothe her. She was obviously too young to know what was going on but was probably feeding off everyone else's emotions. Brandon gestured for Nik to come closer and made room to pull them into the hug with Jeremy as soon as they were close enough.

Nik leaned in and placed a kiss on the side of his head, before turning and doing the same to Jeremy.

Hearing the door opening behind him, Brandon turned to face the medical personnel coming out of the room. A doctor came up to him. "Are you Mrs. Whitaker's family?"

"Yes. We're her children and that's my boyfriend."

"I'm so sorry to tell you that we couldn't revive her. I'm sorry for your loss."

"Mommy go to heaven?"

"Yes, Casey. Your mommy went to heaven, but you've got us now. Okay?"

"Okay." Casey gave a long, shuddering sigh and laid her head back on Nik's shoulder. "I stay wif you."

Brandon spoke to the doctor, at a loss as to what to do now. "Is there anything else we need to do here — or can we go?"

Mrs. Robinson stepped forward. "She took care of all of her funeral arrangements. I'll forward you the email with all the information. I have the keys to your mom's place, so you can get Casey's things for now. You can worry about cleaning out the rest of the apartment later. I can walk out with you, and we can meet there. I know you probably don't have a car seat, so she can ride with me until we get the one from the apartment. She sold her car, so you don't have to worry about that. We can finalize all the paperwork there."

"Okay. Is there a bill or anything I need to take care of?"

"You can worry about that another day. For now, let's get all of you home."

Brandon's shoulders slumped. He wasn't used to this feeling of utter helplessness anymore. He'd made a career of being able to take care of everyone and everything. For now, he decided to follow Mrs. Robinson's advice and get his family home.

Chapter Fifteen

Nikolai let Brandon's hand on his back guide him to the elevator. Brandon had his other arm around Jeremy and was whispering to him as they walked out of the hospital and to the parking lot. Nikolai still held Casey in his arms. She hadn't slept very long earlier. Her head was on his shoulder, but her eyes were wide open. She looked tired but scared she was going to miss something. He was waiting for a total meltdown from her. She had been way too calm so far. Part of that might be exhaustion on her part. He was so excited to get to know her, but hated it came at the death of their mother. Estranged or not, she was still Mom.

Mrs. Robinson unlocked her car and opened the back door where the car seat was located, then turned to speak to Jeremy and Brandon. Nik heard her giving them the apartment address as he went to place Casey in the car seat. Casey came out of her stupor with a vengeance.

"No go! No go! Stay with Brandon, Nik, Jer-my! Mama said!"

"Sh-h, sweetie, sh-h." Nikolai stood and secured his hold on the flailing child, rocking her as he tried to comfort her. Brandon and Jeremy were suddenly on either side of him, and Casey threw herself at Brandon.

Brandon's eyes widened as he caught her. "It's okay, Casey. You're going home with us, but we have to go to your apartment first and get your things. I don't have a car seat for you. We have to get your seat then you can ride with us. Okay?"

Jeremy looked on, visibly distraught that he had no clue what to do, but wanting to do something, as Brandon got Casey to calm down. Brandon's eyes lit up after a moment, an idea obviously coming to him.

"Hey, Casey. How about I ride with you and Mrs. Robinson? I can hold your hand the whole time. Would that be okay? Then we can get your things and you can come home with us. Maybe you can tell me what you want in your bedroom. We can paint it any color you want."

Casey lifted her head and reached for Jeremy this time. "I yike purple."

Brandon ran a hand down Casey's back and kissed the side of her head. "Then purple it shall be. Is it okay if Jeremy rides with you, and we can meet at the apartment?"

Casey vigorously nodded. "We go get Bobo and my crayons."

"Who's Bobo?"

"Bobo is her stuffed monkey. We accidentally left him on the couch while I was getting her out of the door to get to the hospital."

"Bobo's scared. He needs me. We haf to go home and get him."

"Well, you heard her," Nik said. "Let's go, Brandon. We have to get Bobo so he's not scared anymore. See you in a few minutes, kiddo."

Casey waved to them as she let Jeremy put her in her car seat before he walked around the car and got in the back next to her. Jeremy began having an animated conversation with Casey, but Nik couldn't hear what they were talking about with the window closed. Nik tuned into the conversation Brandon and Mrs. Robinson were having in time for them to agree to head out.

Brandon took his hand and led him to the car, giving it a firm squeeze before he released it and went to get in the driver's seat.

Nik climbed in on the passenger side before turning to look at Brandon. "You sure you're up for driving? You've been through a lot in the last hour."

Brandon paused in the act of starting the car to look at Nikolai. "Yeah, I'm good. I mean I'm sad, but I already said goodbye to her a long time ago in my heart." Brandon scrubbed at his face with both hands. "Casey is a shock. It's going to be a huge change. You sure you're on board for all this?"

Nik reached out and cupped Brandon's cheek, making him look at him. "I'm in it for the long haul — good or bad. I think Casey falls firmly in the good category, and I get you. Being with you is worth everything and anything."

Brandon leaned into Nik's touch, closed his eyes and took a deep breath before opening them again. Nik could see the resolve and affection in Brandon's gaze. "Thank you."

"For what?"

"Loving me. Being here for me. Helping me."

"You don't have to thank me for any of that. You make me want to be the best me possible." Nik leaned forward and took Brandon's mouth in a gentle kiss. He pulled back after a moment and reached for his seatbelt. "Now, let's go. We have a girl and all her things to collect."

Brandon turned back to face the front, pressed the button to start the car and put it in drive. "We have a lot to do in the next week or so."

"Yeah. You should call Sergei and let him know you need some time off. He'll be upset if you keep him out of the loop on this."

Brandon's moan in response was amusing, but he clicked the button on his steering wheel and used voice commands to place the call. Sergei answered on the second ring.

"Hello, Brandon. I didn't expect to hear from you today. Is everything all right?"

"Not really, but it will be."

"Is Nikolai okay?" Sergei's voice had a note of panic as he asked the question.

"I'm fine, Sergei," Nikolai cut in.

"Then what's going on? Is one of you pregnant?"

"Ha-ha. Very funny," Nikolai said as drily as he could.

"Well actually, in a way I am," Brandon responded.

Nikolai chuckled at Sergei's shouted "What?"

"My mother just died from complications of breast cancer. She has given me custody of my three-almost-four-year-old sister, Casey."

There was a long pause before Sergei spoke again. "I am sorry for your loss. What are you doing now?"

"Well, we are heading to their apartment to get Casey's things and sign some paperwork with the caseworker, then I am taking her home with me. I need a week to get things figured out."

"You can have as much time as you want, but you will take two weeks at the minimum. You have a room for her?"

"Yeah. I have a guest room, but I just promised her we could paint it purple, and it really isn't set up for a little girl. That's one of the things I'm going to have to do this week."

Nikolai spoke up again. "I'm going to call Kirk next and take this week off too. I'm sure he won't care, once I tell him why."

"Okay. Call me when you are on your way home. We will be there to help." Sergei hung up before either of them could respond.

"Well, we should have expected that." Nikolai choked out on a laugh. Pulling out his own phone, he called Kirk on speaker and quickly told him what was going on.

"Let us know what she needs. We have a bunch of toddler stuff in the attic that we hadn't decided what to do with yet."

"That would be great," Brandon responded. "I get the feeling from Mrs. Robinson that Casey doesn't have a lot, so any help would be appreciated. I guess they recently moved into a smaller place to save some money and for my mom to have less to keep up, since she's been so sick." Brandon paused for a moment. "I really wish she had contacted me sooner. She could have moved in with us instead. It would have given me a chance to get to know Casey beforehand, as well."

"Well, nothing we can do about that now." Kirk's upbeat voice came through the speaker. "We've got your back. Sergei is on the phone with Eric now. It sounds like he is organizing the troops. Eric has talked him into waiting until tomorrow but expect everyone in the morning to meet her and help you get your sister situated."

"Thank you. Yeah, tomorrow is good. We have Jeremy's friends coming over tonight then they are going to Animazement for the day tomorrow."

"Oh, that's right. Are you sure you're still up for all that?"

"Yeah. I think it will be good for Jeremy."

"Probably, but maybe Stuart can take them at least, so you don't have to do it. I know he is helping an artist friend man his booth, so he has to be there."

"That would be great. Let me call him next then. See you tomorrow."

Nikolai hung up his phone as Brandon called Stuart from the car controls. When Stuart answered, they could hear Sergei in the background talking to his mama. He was switching back and forth between English and Russian.

"Uh-oh. Mama H is now on the case."

Brandon and Nik shared a grin. Stuart's chuckle carried over the line. "Yep. She certainly is. You will have a full house tomorrow. Can you shoot us your address, so we know where to go? I don't think anyone has been to your place before. I mean, Sergei could look it up, but that just seems a creepy invasion of privacy. Sadly, I won't be able to stay. I promised a friend I would help them at Animazement tomorrow."

"I'll send the address as soon as we get off the phone. Animazement is actually why we were calling you. We need a favor."

"Sure, what's up?"

"Jeremy and his friends are coming over tonight. The plan was for us to take them to Animazement tomorrow. Could they catch a ride with you?"

"Of course. Not a problem. If the boys don't mind, it would actually be nice for them to help us set up my friend's booth."

"I'm sure they won't care," Brandon interjected. "They're all good kids. Sasha is one of them."

"Oh yeah. Sasha tends to hang with the good ones. Count on me. I can get them back and forth. I'll have them check in with me from time to time as well so I can make sure they are doing okay."

"Yeah. And I'll give you some extra cash in case of emergency."

"Sounds great. That makes me feel a little better. I was feeling bad that I wouldn't be there to help tomorrow."

"Yeah. I think Jeremy will feel a little bad too, but life goes on. He has been looking forward to this forever. I want him to at least do Saturday with his friends."

"Do you have any friends that need passes, Stuart? It doesn't look like Brandon and I will be able to go."

"I think Sasha has a friend who wanted to go and was planning on standing in line tomorrow to get a ticket."

"Oh. that's good to know. I'll talk to him when he gets to the house tonight." Nikolai saw that Mrs. Robinson had pulled into the parking lot of a tired and rundown apartment complex. "It appears we've made it to their apartment. Let me talk to you later."

"Sounds good. Tell the boys I will pick them up at eight tomorrow morning."

"Will do. Thanks, Stuart."

"Anytime, Nik. You're family, after all."

"Thanks from me and Jeremy too, Stuart."

"Same goes, butthead. You're family too. Got it?"

Nik watched as Brandon appeared to be hit right in the feels with Stuart's comment. "Got it," he choked out.

"See you tomorrow."

"Later."

"Well," Brandon sighed, looking out of the window and watching Jeremy get Casey out of her car seat. "We're here."

"Yep. On to our next grand adventure." Nik tried to keep his tone upbeat and not show how horrified he was by the state of the apartment complex where they were. "We better get inside and get Casey's things."

"The sooner the better. I don't think I want to be here after dark."

"Oh, man. Thank you for saying that. Me neither."

"Glad we're on the same page. Let's get this done."

Brandon and Nik got out of the car and joined the others waiting for them at the bottom of the steps. Casey waved to them when they got close then held her arms up for Brandon to carry her. "We gotta go up and up and up to get to the partment."

"Do we now?" Nik looked at Mrs. Robinson for clarification.

Mrs. Robinson winced. "Yeah. They're on the fourth floor. It's just a small studio, so there isn't much."

Making the trek up the stairs, Nik listened as Casey told Brandon a story about her best friend at preschool.

"Where does she go to school, Mrs. Robinson?"

"I'll have to look at the file, but I think it's a daycare center nearby."

Nik turned to look at Mrs. Robinson with a raised brow. Mrs. Robinson winced. "Yeah. I know she won't still be going there. I'll get you the information so you can call and withdraw her."

"I think that would be best." As they turned to go up the final set of stairs, Nik tried to ignore the smell of marijuana permeating the stairway. "Was the apartment rented furnished or do we need to get everything out?"

"It wasn't rented furnished, but there honestly isn't much in there that you likely want. There's a couch and a mattress on the floor, some clothes and a few dishes."

"Really?"

"Yeah. I think she sold almost everything when they downsized."

Mrs. Robinson pulled out a set of keys and opened the apartment door, then they all followed her inside. Nik looked around in shocked horror. Mrs. Robinson had *not* been exaggerating. There was hardly anything in the apartment. In one corner were some plastic crates with clothes folded and stacked in them. There was a mattress on the floor and two barstools at the counter, but no dining table. Casey was on a torn and battered, flowered couch with Jeremy, showing him Bobo, but Nik didn't see any other toys or even a television. He did see an old laptop on the counter in the kitchen, but that was the extent of the electronics in the house.

"Wow." Brandon looked at Nik in horror.

"Yeah. I think we can probably grab everything in one trip here. I'm not sure what to do about the couch and mattress. We don't need them, and they've honestly seen better days."

"Better days," Brandon scoffed. "I don't think I've seen a couch that ugly before. When was it made? The seventies?"

"No idea."

"I'll tell you what. Why don't you go ahead and pack up everything we're taking, and I'll go talk to the building manager. I saw his door when we came in. Maybe he has someone who wants the apartment and needs the couch and mattress."

"Good idea. See you in a few minutes." Nik grabbed and squeezed Brandon's hand to stop him as he went to pass by him. When Brandon looked at him in question, Nik leaned in and gave him a kiss. "We got this."

Brandon searched his eyes for a moment then leaned their foreheads together for a moment. "Yeah." He pulled Nik in for a brief hug before letting go and walking away to head down the stairs.

"Okay." Nik clapped his hands together, getting everyone's attention. "Jeremy, I need you to see if you can find some garbage bags in the kitchen for the bedding. Casey, why don't you help me with the clothes? Mrs. Robinson," he called out to where Mrs. Robinson was in the kitchen, "Brandon will be right back. He went to talk to the apartment manager real quick to see if there is any way we can be done here once we leave."

Mrs. Robinson nodded to him then went back to pulling things out of the cupboards. "There's only a quart of milk and a bottle of juice in the refrigerator — and some butter and ketchup."

"Yeah. If you could go ahead and toss those things. We don't need them."

Casey paused in her story to Jeremy about Bobo. "Can I have some juice, Nik?"

"Sure. Mrs. Robinson, is there a cup for Casey to have some juice?"

"Yep. I'll get her some."

"Great. Jeremy, did you find garbage bags?"

"Yep."

"Fantastic. You bag up the dirty bedding and clothes in the corner there and hand me another bag for your mom's clothes. Do we need to worry about picking an outfit for the funeral home?"

"No funeral planned. She simply wants to be buried next to her husband."

"All righty then. We'll need to see whether Brandon and Jeremy want to have a memorial service of some kind, even if it's just a graveside thing, but we can talk about that later." Nik knelt down next to the clothing crates. He took the ones with Casey's clothes and laid them on their backs. They would be easy to carry that way. There were only two, so that made it simpler. Another crate held crayons, coloring books and a few storybooks, and that crate got stacked with Casey's clothes.

"Casey, do you want to color while we get your things together?"

"Yes, please."

Nik grabbed a coloring book and small box of crayons and set them up for the little girl, then he went back and emptied the other clothes into one of the garbage bags. Once that was done, he took the three empty crates into the kitchen to use to pack up the items there.

Mrs. Robinson had pulled everything out of the cupboards. There wasn't a lot—two different sized frying pans and one saucepan, four each of plates and bowls, one additional plastic cup and some silverware. From the pantry came blue boxes of mac and cheese mixes, along with some ramen noodle packets and an unopened bag of rice. "Mrs. Robinson, is there anyone you know who could use this stuff?" Nik waved a hand to encompass everything on the counter.

"There are always families who could use it. None of the food is open, so that's good."

Nik nodded. "Let's load it all in one of the crates then and we can carry it down to the car for you. Anything in the freezer?"

"Nope."

"Jeremy, can you check the closet there, while I go through the bathroom?"

"Sure thing, Nik."

Nik took another crate into the bathroom, but there wasn't much there, either — one bottle of shampoo and a tube of toothpaste, along with their toothbrushes. Nothing was in any of the drawers other than a first-aid kit. There were four towels. Two were drying on the towel rack and two lay folded up on a shelf. He put the clean towels on the bottom of the crate before putting the shampoo and first-aid kit on top. The adult toothbrush and toothpaste went into the trash can, but he grabbed the kid's toothbrush and toothpaste and set it next to the shampoo. The toothbrush had seen better days and would have to be added to the list of things to get her, but it would do for now. Nik carried the crate and trash can out to the living area and was putting the dirty towels into the dirty clothes bag when Brandon returned.

"How's it going up here?"

"I got juice, Brandon!"

Brandon walked over and ran a hand over her curls. "I'm glad, sweetie. You doing okay?"

Casey nodded. "Yep. I gots Bobo and juice."

Brandon leaned down and placed a kiss on top of her head. "Good. How about the rest of you?"

"I honestly think we're almost done. Jeremy, what did you find in the closet?"

"Casey's car seat and a couple of jackets. That's it. I put Mom's jacket in the bag with all her clothes after I checked the pockets. I put Casey's in her crate, although it looks too little already. I found a little safe with all their personal papers in it too. I put it on the counter, there."

Mrs. Robinson joined the conversation. "Kitchen is done. What did the manager say?"

Brandon scowled. "He said he had someone who wanted the apartment, but if we leave items and don't clean, there's a two-hundred-fifty-dollar fee we would have to pay."

Nik looked around the apartment. "Worth it."

Brandon smirked. "That's what I said. I Paypal'd him the money and got a receipt. He'll be up in a few minutes to get the keys. How much longer do you think we'll be?"

"Five minutes. Jeremy, let's start taking the crates downstairs. Brandon, can I have your keys?"

"Sure. Here you go. We'll stack everything in the hall, so we can make our way out."

"Great. Be back in a few." Nik and Jeremy loaded up with the filled crates and made their way downstairs.

"Nik," Jeremy began hesitantly once they reached the car, and Nik had popped the trunk and loaded the crates into the open space.

"What's up, buddy?" Nik had only a moment to prepare before he had an armful of emotional teenager.

"This sucks—all but the Casey part," he added quickly. "I'm so lucky I've had Brandon." Jeremy lost it then, and all Nik could do was hold Jeremy as he cried, rubbing his back and swaying him side to side a little. Eventually the crying stopped, and Jeremy slumped in his arms. "How embarrassing."

Nik leaned back a little. "Look at me, Jeremy." Nik waited until Jeremy made eye contact. "There is nothing embarrassing about you crying. You've had a lot thrown at you this afternoon." Nik paused to glance at his watch. "God, it's only four. We didn't even get to the hospital until one. You have been a trooper and a great big brother. You looked out for your sister and rode with her so she would stay calm, and you've worked hard to help us get her out of this apartment. You have nothing, absolutely nothing to be ashamed of. Got me?" Jeremy nodded. "All righty then. Let's grab some napkins out of the car so you can pull yourself together. Maybe use some water from one of the water bottles to clean off your face. You stay with the car, and I'll go get another load of stuff. Okay?"

"Yeah. Thanks, Nik."

"Hey, that's what family is for. Right?"

"Right," Jeremy nodded decisively.

"Why don't you use this time to call Jessie and let him know what is going on. I'm sure Sasha knows by now."

"Good idea."

Nik waited until Jeremy pulled out his phone before dashing up the stairs and back to the apartment. There was one more crate of the kitchen stuff going into Mrs. Robinson's car and the garbage bags of clothes and the car seat. That's all that was left other than the little safe and the papers Mrs. Robinson and Brandon were currently going over—a life packed up in one afternoon.

Chapter Sixteen

Brandon walked through the apartment space one more time after placing the remaining crate and car seat out in the hall. That was it. Mrs. Robinson waved him over to the kitchen counter, where she had pulled paperwork out of her case.

"We just have a few more items to go over. I was going to contact you on Monday to get the ball rolling. Unfortunately, time obviously wasn't on our side. I'll call you once I have a date to go in front of the judge for the adoption. All the paperwork is done, but you might want your lawyer to go over it with you. For now, I am releasing custody of Casey to you. This paperwork is the proof you need for adding her to your insurance, etc. Mrs. Whitaker made a list of all the information for Casey on this sheet. Here is the phone number for her day care and pediatrician. Her birth certificate, social security card and immunization records she said were in the safe. Your mother's information is on this separate sheet. All her personal records are also in the safe."

Brandon nodded. "Thank you for your help today. I appreciate you taking time out of your schedule to do so."

"Casey and your mom were my schedule today. We were making the plan for reaching out to you, as I said."

"Well, you've gone above and beyond, and I appreciate it."

"You're doing a great job with Jeremy, and I'm sure you're going to do the same with Casey."

"I hope so. I'll do my best, at any rate."

"That's all any parent can do, and it sounds like you have a great support network. Nik was telling us as we worked about all the people coming over tomorrow to help you get her settled."

Brandon shrugged. "We're family."

Mrs. Robinson laid a hand on his arm. "And you've made a great one. Hold on to that as you move forward. I've also put a list of family counsellors in the packet. It might not hurt for all of you to talk to someone. This is going to be a huge adjustment."

Brandon nodded again. "We already have someone. We started going after I got custody of Jeremy."

"Great. Then I'm preaching to the choir. Now, how about we get out of here?

"Yeah." Brandon turned his head when he heard a noise at the door. "Hey, where's Jeremy?"

"He needed a minute."

Brandon felt alarm go through him and took a step toward Nik. "Is he okay?"

Nik held up a hand. "He will be. He just got overwhelmed for a minute. Did the apartment manager come up already?"

"Yep. He was in and out in two minutes. We're all set."

"Okay then, let's get the rest of this stuff and blow this popsicle stand. I'm sure everyone is getting hungry by now."

"Yay, food!" Casey cheered from the barstool.

"Yep." Brandon stepped back and lifted her from her seat and set her on the floor, before handing her Bobo. "Do you think you can carry your crayons and Bobo?"

"Yep. I'm a big girl. I help."

"Great. Here you go. Now hold Mrs. Robinson's hand while we go down the stairs. Okay?"

"Yep. Yep."

Mrs. Robinson scooped up the plastic cup Casey had been drinking out of and put it in the crate with all the other items. "I'll wash everything when I get back to the office."

"Sounds good. I'm probably going to need you to show me how to put in the car seat. I have no clue."

"Well at least you have a newer car, so it will be easier, but I'll show you."

"Thanks."

"Yeah. Tanks, Mrs. Obinson. Gotta be safe."

Casey looked so serious as she talked to Mrs. Robinson that Brandon couldn't help but laugh. "Yes, Casey. We gotta be safe."

They all scooped up the rest of the items then closed the door behind them before making their way down the stairs and to the cars. Nik and Jeremy stuffed the plastic bags in around the crates and stashed the other crate in Mrs. Robinson's car, while Mrs. Robinson gave Brandon a lesson in how to install the car seat.

Mrs. Robinson went down on one knee and hugged Casey once they were done. "Be good for Brandon, Nik and Jeremy, okay?"

"Yep. We go see Mommy later, right?"

There was a long pause while everyone looked at each other helplessly. Brandon scooped Casey up so he could hold her as he talked. "I'm sorry, Casey, but Mommy is gone. We won't be able to go see her anymore."

Tears filled Casey's eyes as she stared at Brandon in horror. "Where'd Mommy go?"

"Mommy was very sick. She went to heaven, sweetie. You're going to come live with Jeremy and me now. We're going to be your family."

"Oh," she sobbed, "no more Mommy?" She started to cry harder. Brandon didn't know what to do other than hold her and wait her out. Once she calmed, he tried to explain things again.

"Mommy was very sick, and she had to go to heaven, but I'm going to be your daddy and Jeremy is going to be your big brother and Nik is going to be your papa."

Brandon saw Nik jerk in surprise out of the corner of his eye.

"I'll have *two* daddies?" Casey held up two fingers as she asked the question.

"Yep. Two daddies and a big brother. Okay?"

"Okay." Casey laid her head on Brandon's shoulder with an exhausted sigh.

"Let's go home."

"We eat?"

"Yep. How about we stop at McDonald's and get some food. We're going to have pizza later, okay? Jeremy has some friends coming over to play."

"I like pizza and chicken nuggets."

"Then it's a plan. Let's get you in your car seat then we'll go get McDonald's. Maybe you can take a little nap with Bobo until we get home."

"Okay. Bobo's tired."

"I'm sure he is." Brandon strapped her into the seat and pressed a kiss to the top of her head before gently closing the door. Nik stepped forward and pulled Brandon into his arms for a much, needed hug. "Man, this sucks so hard," he whispered in Nik's ear.

"I know, babe," Nik whispered back. "But you're doing a great job. Let's get her home."

Brandon squeezed him tight one more time before letting go and walking over to Mrs. Robinson. He stuck his hand out to her for a shake. "Thank you again for all your time today."

"No problem. As I said, have your lawyer review the documents, and I will let you know when we get the adoption proceeding scheduled. Here's my card for you to give to your lawyer in case they have any questions."

"Okay. Will do."

"And, Brandon, the offer is open for you too. If you ever have any questions, please let me know."

"Thank you." Brandon pointed a thumb back in the direction of his car. "I'm going to get everyone home then we will evaluate everything from there. I think I actually need to sleep on it tonight and hit it tomorrow."

"Probably for the best. Enjoy your family. I like your Nik. You picked a good one there."

"Thanks. I think so too."

With a final wave, Mrs. Robinson got in her car and drove away. Brandon got into the car and sat there for a minute, trying to remember what he was supposed to do next. Nik's hand on his arm startled him.

"You okay? Do you need me to drive?"

Brandon thought for a moment. "Yeah. You probably should. I'm all over the place at the moment."

"Okay."

They switched places, Nik's quick hand-squeeze as they passed each other in front of the car allowed Brandon to take another deep breath and the overwhelming swell of emotion receded a little bit. Once in the car and strapped in, he turned to look at Casey, who was already asleep in her seat, then Jeremy. Jeremy's eyes were a little red, like he had been crying.

"You okay, Jeremy?"

Jeremy shrugged. "I will be. I lost it all over Nik a bit ago. I guess that means we're keeping him."

Nik snorted as he reversed out of the parking spot. "The Whitaker version of licking something and claiming it? Except you got snot on me instead?"

"Yep. I did it. Casey did it. Brandon's next."

"I'm okay with that. Whatever you guys need." Nik grabbed Brandon's hand and raised it to his lips. "As long as I get to keep you guys right back."

"Always." Brandon twined their fingers together and held on tight.

Nik cleared his throat. "Papa?"

"If you want."

"Oh, I want."

"Good. I'll call the lawyer and make an appointment. We'll get your name on the paperwork too, if we can."

"Does this mean Nik's moving in with us?"

"It means I'd like him to...but no pressure."

Nik scoffed. "You think I don't want that? I just agreed to adopt a kid with you."

"Good. It's a plan then. When do the boys get to our place again?"

"Not until seven now. I wasn't sure how long we were going to be, so I pushed it back a bit. By the way, Sergei can't wait to meet Casey, so he offered to ride with Mama H to our place to drop Sasha off. I guess there was a whole discussion. Mama H and Sergei both wanted to be the first to meet her. This was their compromise.

Brandon couldn't hold back his laughter. "That's funny."

"Right?"

"That's so Sergei," Nik sighed. "Mr. Nosy Pants."

"Hey, there's a McDonald's. You told Casey we'd get her nuggets."

Nik turned on the blinker. "On it. What does everybody want?"

Luckily the line wasn't long, and they were soon back on the road. Casey woke up when she smelled the food and was clutching her Happy Meal box with one hand while eating nuggets and French fries with her other hand, Bobo in the crook of her arm.

Brandon waited until she swallowed her current mouthful before speaking to her. "Slow down, Casey. No one's going to take away your chicken nuggets. I don't want you to choke."

"Okay, Brandon. I sorry."

"It's okay, sweetie. We'll be home soon. We have more food there if you're still hungry, and we'll order pizza later. All right?"

"Yummy. I like pizza."

"Yeah? What kind do you like?"

"Cheese and peppernonis."

"Pepperoni?" Brandon thought it was adorable how she added the extra n.

"Yep. Peppernonis are yummy."

"We'll make sure to get a pepperoni pizza, then."

"You know most places have kid's meals. We can check and see if the place you order from has one."

"Oh yeah. I forgot about those. Jeremy hasn't ordered from the kid's meal from the time I got him."

"True statement. I like food."

"Really? We didn't know. It's so subtle," Nik teased.

Sneaking a glance at Casey, Brandon saw that she had fallen back asleep with a half-eaten nugget clenched in her hand. "Jeremy, could you rescue the nugget and put it back in the box?"

"Yep."

Jeremy grabbed the nugget and closed the Happy Meal box back up, as Nik turned into their subdivision then into their driveway.

Brandon took a deep breath. "We can do this."

"Yep. We got this, bro."

Nik just smiled at him.

Let the adventure begin.

Chapter Seventeen

Nik unbuckled and carried the still-sleeping Casey into the house and laid her on the couch. Grabbing the blanket off the back, he covered her with it then went out to help Brandon and Jeremy bring stuff in. They managed to get everything out of the car and into the house in one trip with all three of them doing it. Jeremy ran upstairs to his room for some downtime before his friends got there. Brandon snagged all the paperwork and took it to his office to go over later, while Nik sat on the floor to start going through all Casey's clothes to see what they had to work with. It wasn't a lot.

"We're going to need to go on a shopping trip with Casey," Nik told Brandon upon his return. "Most of these clothes are either stained or worn—and that's assuming some of it even fits her. They look a little small. I don't know a lot about little girl clothes, though."

"I figured that, based on the number of items in the apartment. That was..." Brandon's expression was bleak as he paused, obviously not knowing how to finish that sentence.

"Yeah. That was... I think we're going to have to take her with us and have her try on clothes, since I have no idea about sizing. I've found three different sizes in this stack."

"Kirk and Eric may be able to help with that tomorrow. They both have experience with their girls." Brandon scrubbed his face with his hands. "This is a lot. I have so many things to do that I don't even know where to start."

"Well, why don't you get a pen and paper and make your usual lists? That will help you. You know it will."

"You're right." Brandon stood and placed a kiss on the top of Nik's head as he passed by.

Nik collected the salvageable items and took them to the washing machine. He grabbed the dirty towels and sheets to throw in at the same time. To think that not even twelve hours ago, he was worried about what costume to wear to Animazement. Nik could only shake his head to himself, life had a tendency to show what was important in dramatic ways.

Nik went to Brandon's office and found him hunched over his desk rapidly scribbling. He leaned against the doorframe and just watched his boyfriend for a few minutes. He must have made some sound because Brandon raised his head.

"What's up?"

"I was standing here thinking about how lucky I am to have you in my life."

"Come here," Brandon commanded, pushing his chair away from his desk and holding out his hand.

Nik crossed the room and straddled Brandon's lap, looping his arms around Brandon's neck. Brandon wrapped his arms around him, buried his nose in Nik's throat and held on. Nik felt a shudder go through him. "It's okay, Brandon. I've got you."

That was it. The floodgates opened and Brandon lost it. Nik felt the dampness of tears on his shirt for the third time that day. Nik petted Brandon, running his hand down the back of Brandon's head and down as far as he could reach, over and over, until Brandon finally calmed and sighed deeply.

"It will be okay, babe. You've got a great support system in place. That little girl is going to be so loved, though I *am* sorry about the way this all happened. I know losing your mom was hard, no matter how estranged you were."

Brandon nodded against his neck. "It hurt more than I expected. I thought my heart was going to break right in two when Casey asked to go see her mommy."

Nik tightened his arms around Brandon's shoulders. "Yeah. That was a tough one. You handled it so well, though. You've handled everything so well, and hey, now I've been fully claimed by all the Whitakers."

Brandon snorted a laugh into Nik's neck, making Nik wiggle when it tickled. "Thanks for hanging in there with me today."

"Hey. I'm not going anywhere. After all the work I've put into stalking you, you think I'm going to let you get away now?"

"Well, as Jeremy said, you've been claimed."

Nik got serious again. "We do have to talk about the papa thing. Are you sure about that? We haven't been together that long."

Brandon leaned far enough away so he could make eye contact with Nik. "I'm very sure about all of it. I want you to adopt her with me. I want you to move in here with us and maybe more sometime in the future."

Nik released the breath he had been holding as he waited for Brandon's response. "I can get behind that plan."

"Good. Now, can you let me go get cleaned up and maybe change my shirt before everyone gets here?" Brandon paused to give Nik a quick once over as well, before wincing. "You might want to change your shirt too."

Glancing down, Nik saw that his shirt was now a soaked and wrinkled mess, in addition to being dirty and sweaty from the day. He groaned. "Yeah. Sounds like a plan. I might jump in the shower real quick as well."

"That sounds like a great idea. Let me go see if Jeremy can keep an ear out for Casey — and maybe I'll join you."

"Best offer I've had today."

Nik grabbed a change of clothes and took them into the bathroom. He turned on the water to let it warm while he used the toilet. Jumping in the shower, the feel of the water pounding on his body made him moan and helped wash away some of the day's stress. The shower door opened, and he was hit with a wave of cold air, followed by his boyfriend wrapping him in his arms.

"This has a been a long day."

Nikolai chuckled. "I was just thinking the same thing, but we're getting through it."

Brandon bent his head and gave Nikolai a thorough kiss, eventually pulling away to yawn. "Man, was it only lunchtime that we made out in your apartment?" Brandon thunked his head onto Nik's shoulder. "This afternoon has felt like a week."

Nik ran his hands over Brandon in a soothing motion. "It has been quite eventful." Nik reached for the shampoo, poured some into his hand and started gently working it through Brandon's hair. "Tilt your head back, babe."

Brandon groaned as he let Nik strip the shampoo out of his hair. "That feels good."

"That's what I was going for." Once he was satisfied that he got all the shampoo out, he reached for the washcloth and soap, cleaning his boyfriend from top to bottom, leaving the best parts for last. Dropping to his knees, Nik soaped up the washcloth and ran it up and down Brandon's hardening length.

"Are you going to do something about that or just tease me?"

"I'm hungry." Nik took a moment to rinse Brandon off before putting his mouth where the washcloth had been, immediately taking Brandon to the root. Running his tongue along the vein on the bottom, he smiled as that made Brandon gasp, grab his head in his hands and buck his hips. Nik pulled off with a slurp, saying, "Fuck my mouth. Take what you need."

Brandon looked down at him for a moment before he tentatively pushed his hips forward. Nik pressed up to meet him. After a few strokes, Brandon paused to reposition his grip on Nik's head then started making deeper harder strokes. Nik lowered one of his hands to start stroking his own hard erection. With the other, he reached behind and pressed a soapy finger into Brandon's opening.

Nik was already close to the edge. Being used by Brandon was a total turn-on. A half-dozen strokes later, Brandon's hips stuttered, and he was coming. Nik pulled back enough so he could taste Brandon's unique flavor on his tongue. The scent and taste, along with the pulsing around his finger still in Brandon's hole, sent Nik over the edge. He had to pull off Brandon's cock to get some much-needed oxygen into his lungs.

Nik laid his head against Brandon's thigh for a moment, catching his breath. He grabbed the washcloth and soap again and gently washed Brandon. Standing up made Nik groan. "Man, tiles are not good on the knees."

Brandon didn't say anything, just pulled Nik into his arms and kissed him lazily. "I love you. Thank you for making a horrific day better."

"Love you too, babe." With a sigh, Nik pulled out of Brandon's arms. "Rinse off and then you better get out there. Sergei, Mama H and the boys should be here soon. One of us should be downstairs to meet them. Let me wash up fast then I'll join you."

"You don't want me to return the favor and wash you?"

"I'll take a raincheck. I wouldn't be surprised if they were early, since they know we're home already."

"Okay. I'm on it." Brandon leaned in for one more kiss before he left Nik to finish on his own.

Nik washed up and got out of the shower, drying off in time to hear the doorbell ring. He brushed his hair and threw it up into a messy ponytail, then put on his clean clothes, pulling on his shirt as he walked out of the door.

After descending the stairs, he met absolute chaos. The boys were having an energetic discussion about what they hoped to see at the convention the next day. Mama H was facing Brandon and holding his hands tightly in her own, obviously giving him a pep talk, while Sergei was holding Casey and they were having an animated conversation about something to do with kittens and dragons and...goldfish?

"Sergei, you are not buying her a pet right now." The two turned matching pouting expressions on Nik. "I mean it. Not right now. We have a lot to sort out. A pet can wait."

Mama H interrupted before Sergei could say anything. "Listen to your cousin, Sergei. They don't need a pet right now." Short pause. "It would make a wonderful Christmas present, though. We will discuss later."

Nikolai threw his hands up in disgust. "You two are impossible."

"What? Mama is right. That will give us time to research the best options. Right, *milochka*?"

"What dat mean?"

"Hmm-m. The closest in English is 'sweetie pie'. You want to be my sweetie pie?"

Casey nodded rapidly. "I be your sweetie pie, Unca Siryay."

"Unca Siryay?" Nik questioned with amusement.

Sergei shrugged. "She is having a little difficulty with my name. It's all good."

Brandon walked over and slid his arm around Nikolai's waist. "Looking a little wild-eyed there, babe. Everything okay?" Nikolai asked.

"Yeah. Mama H was giving me a pep talk and reminding me that I have a family that will help — and not to forget it."

Nik leaned in and gave Brandon a kiss on his cheek. "And you've got me."

Brandon turned his head and stared into Nikolai's eyes for a moment. "I'm counting on that, most of all."

Brandon started to lean in to kiss Nikolai but was interrupted by the boys joining them.

"When can we order pizza? We're starving." Jeremy's pathetic moan at the end made Nik laugh.

"You just ate like two hours ago."

"Dude, that was two whole hours ago."

"I get peppernonis. Right, Brandon?"

"Right, princess." Brandon held out his arms for Casey, and she willingly came to him and threw her arms around his neck. He gave her a hug before handing her to Mama H. "Mama H was complaining she didn't get to hold you yet, because Uncle Sergei picked you up first."

Nikolai laughed at the look of total disgruntlement on Sergei's face. "You have to share, Sergei."

"I suppose," Sergei said with a huge put-upon sigh.

"You and Stuart should get your own."

Sergei's eyes lit up. "We are in discussions for a year or two down the road. We want to make sure our relationship is solid before we add kids to the mix, but soon. There are a lot of kids out there who need homes, so we're not sure if we want to go the adoption or surrogate route."

"Yeah. While that would have been the ideal, Nik and I don't have that luxury, unfortunately."

"Communication and respect," Mama H declared. "Those are the things that will get you through any difficulties. Remember that."

"Yes, ma'am."

"Good boy." Mama H patted Brandon on the cheek, before handing Casey off. "Now, we should get going so they can get some pizza ordered for these poor, starving teenagers. They might waste away if they aren't fed soon."

"Your sarcasm game is strong tonight, Mama," Sasha said as he came over, picked up his mother and twirled around with her in his arms.

Casey clapped her hands in excitement. "Do me! Do me!"

"Now see what you started, young man?"

Sasha just laughed, scooped up Casey and spun her in a circle before shouting "Airplane," and switching his hold so she was perpendicular to the floor with one of his hands under her legs and the other under her chest. "Arms out!" Once she complied, he started zooming her around the room, buzzing Jeremy and Jessie as he went by them. Their combined giggles made all the adults laugh at their antics.

Brandon clapped his hands. "Enough now. Let's get the pizzas ordered. Mama H, do you want to stay for dinner?"

"I'm sure you have things to get organized and figured out before the horde descends tomorrow."

"Yeah, and that's why it would be good if you stayed. We need to talk to Casey about what she wants in her room, and since I have no experience with little girls, any advice and help would be welcome."

Casey came running up and wrapped her arms around Brandon's legs. "Purple. I yike purple."

Brandon ran his hand down the back of Casey's head. "We know sweetie. We'll paint your room purple. Okay?"

"Yay! Jer-my! Jer-my! My room gonna be purple!"

"I heard. That's going to be so fun."

"Yay!" Casey started jumping up and down in her excitement.

Nikolai scooped her up, laughing. "Yes. It's exciting, and we have friends coming to help, so hopefully you will have a purple room by tomorrow afternoon. Okay?"

"Yep."

"Good. Now let's order some pizza."

Chapter Eighteen

Brandon stretched as he woke up and moved over to snuggle with his boyfriend to find that he was the only one currently in the bed. Looking at the clock, he saw it was just six a.m. *Where is he?* He went to the bathroom and threw on some sweats over the boxers he had slept in and grabbed a T-shirt. Following the voices he could hear once he opened the bedroom door, Brandon went down to the kitchen. Standing in the doorway his heart melted at the scene in front of him.

Casey was sitting on Nik's lap at the breakfast bar, working her way through a frozen waffle, while Nik read to her from one of her books. She giggled as Nik did different voices for all the characters in the story. His chuckle gave him away, and two heads turned to look at him.

"Hi, Brandon. We're having beckfast."

"I see that. Is it good?"

Casey nodded. "Yummy."

Brandon walked closer, leaned down and kissed the top of her head. "I'm surprised you can fit any waffles in there after all the pizza you ate last night."

Casey giggled again, and Brandon leaned forward again to kiss Nik. "Morning. What are you two doing up so early, anyway?"

"Morning. Casey woke up about an hour ago and was a little scared, so she came into our room. You didn't even move when she climbed in with us. We decided to let you sleep, since it's going to be a very busy time. Jessie wanted some help with his makeup for today, anyway, so this way I'm fully awake when he's ready for me." Nik held up his coffee cup to indicate he was drinking caffeine to help in that regard.

"Do you have everything you need?"

Nik just gave him a long look until Brandon realized what he had asked. "Duh. Stupid question. Do you want me to watch her while you go upstairs, get dressed and grab your supplies?"

"That's probably a good idea." He stood up and lowered Casey onto the bar stool they had been sharing. "I hear the boys starting to move around. You might want to get her dressed for the day and brush her teeth once she's done with breakfast. Just a heads up, a new toothbrush is on the list for her. Her current one has seen better days."

"A princess one. Right, Nik?"

"Right, kiddo."

"Sounds like a plan. I'll get her ready, then I'll get dressed for the day and brush my teeth too." Brandon grabbed Nik's arm and gave him a quick kiss before he left. Nik smiled at him as they pulled apart.

"We got this."

"Yep. We've got a plan, at any rate—now let's see how well we can execute it."

Nik just laughed as he went up the stairs.

"What?" Brandon yelled after him.

"You've got a child under five now. Good luck having anything go exactly to plan."

"I thought you were Mister Positivity..."

Laughter was Nik's only response.

"Brandon! Help! The book is trying to *eat* me." Turning back to Casey, he found her shaking the book, trying to get it loose. She had obviously touched it with her sticky, syrup-covered hand and the page was now stuck to her fingers.

"Hold on. Hold on." Brandon grabbed Casey's wrist to stop her flailing and moved her hand and the book to the counter, where he gently peeled her fingers from the page. "You can't touch paper with sticky hands, baby girl."

"Oh. Okay. Thank you. We go see Mommy now?"

Brandon sucked in a breath. "No, baby girl. Mommy is in heaven. We can't see her anymore. You're going to live here with me, and Jeremy and Nik. I'm going to be your daddy. Remember?"

Casey's eyes filled with tears. "I can't have a daddy *and* a mommy?"

Brandon picked Casey up and cradled her in his arms. "No, baby. Just a daddy. Two daddies, actually. Nik will be your papa. Isn't that special?

Casey nodded where she had it buried in the crook of his neck. "I miss Mommy."

"I know, baby, but you have lots of family now. Everyone is going to love you, and I will do my very best for you. Okay?" Casey nodded again. "Let's go get you cleaned up and ready for the day. We have people coming soon to help make your room perfect."

"Purple."

"Yep. Lots of purple."

Nikolai passed them on the stairs. "Hey, do you think we should run out and grab snacks and drinks and things for everyone? The boys decimated the snack supply last night."

"Mama H said she was going to bring breakfast for everyone. We can order something for lunch."

"Okay. Should have known you had a plan."

"Yep. I'm going to get Casey ready for the day, then I'll be back down."

"I'll come up and help after I drop this stuff off downstairs. The boys aren't ready for me yet."

Brandon brushed Casey's teeth and hair and washed off all the sticky syrup and leftover tears before returning to Casey's bedroom to meet Nikolai. Nik had Casey's clothes laid out, so it was simply a matter of getting her dressed before they headed downstairs.

"By the way, Nik. I spoke to the lawyer Sergei recommended last night and sent him the will I found in my mother's safe, as well as all the paperwork from Mrs. Robinson. He is starting the process on everything. There are still steps to complete, even with the will, though. He will work with Mrs. Robinson to get things moving as quickly as possible. He needs your information ASAP to add you to the adoption petition."

"Sure. Send me the number, and I'll call him after the holiday. I'm assuming he isn't working this weekend."

"No. He said Tuesday is fine. He has plenty of other things to work on in the meantime."

"Great."

They walked into the kitchen where the boys were congregated, making breakfast.

"Hey, Nik! Do you think you could help me with my ears after you help Jessie with his makeup?"

"Sure. I have a product I use with some of my drag queen friends that works fantastically with prosthetics. Your ears shouldn't come off until you want to take them off."

"Awesome!" Jeremy bounced on his toes a few times before turning back to the bacon he was cooking. "This looks like it's done. How are the eggs coming, Bones?"

"Just finishing up."

Brandon saw Casey looking confused. "What's the matter, Casey?"

"I don't see any bones. Where are they?"

Sasha came over to Casey and booped her on the nose. "That's my nickname. My friends call me Bones."

"Can I call you Bones?"

"Are we friends?"

Casey nodded excitedly.

"Then you can call me Bones."

"Yay!"

Everyone laughed at Casey's excitement. Brandon caught Nik's eye and felt a warm glow when he gave him a wink. *Family.*

Nik was just finishing Jessie's makeup when the doorbell rang. Brandon was glad Jeremy offered to get the door, because he was too busy staring at Jessie's transformation. Jessie's delicate features and high cheekbones were even more pronounced with the way Nikolai had applied everything. He was setting the wig on Jessie's head when they were invaded.

"Wow," Stuart said from next to Brandon. "Nik does good work. You look amazing, Jessie."

"Can I go look now?" Jessie asked.

"Yep. Go ahead. I'm done. Jeremy, come on over and let's get those ears on." Jeremy hopped up into the chair, and Nik made quick work of getting the Vulcan-ears applied. "There. All done."

"You guys all ready?" Three yesses answered Stuart. "Let's rock and roll then, gentlemen. My friend is waiting for us."

They all started to exit the kitchen, but Jessie paused at the doorway and ran back to give Nik a quick hug. "Thank you so much. I look so good. I couldn't have done it as well."

"Anytime. It's kinda my thing. Make sure you guys get pictures. Your mom is going to want to see."

"I sent some selfies from the bathroom."

"Good job."

Brandon stepped forward after nonchalantly handing Stuart some extra cash, just in case. "Bye, boys. Have fun but stay out of trouble. Call if you need anything or find Stuart, since he will be there all day as well."

"Thanks. Later, Bro."

"Bye, Jer-my," Casey shouted from her spot on the couch, where she was watching cartoons. "See ya laters, alligators!"

"In a while, crocodile," all three boys answered her. Casey then dissolved into giggles and was still giggling when they left.

"Was Stuart the only one here so far?"

"Yeah. He said Sergei and his mother are five minutes out. The others are not far behind them."

"Great. I was thinking...maybe your mama and I could take Casey clothes shopping and grab some drinks, snacks and such at the same time, while you guys get started. She needs everything, and I really don't think it can wait."

Brandon gave a long sigh. "Yeah. I like that plan. I was trying to figure out when we could do that, and I was honestly a little concerned about how we were going to keep her from getting underfoot."

"Yeah. Well, it will probably take a couple hours to shop, and Lee is bringing the paint and painting supplies. He said that would be his and Saul's contribution. The room's not that big. It probably won't take that long to paint."

"You're right. Let's do that." Any further conversation was halted by the ringing of the doorbell, again. Opening the door, Brandon found that everyone had arrived at the same time. "Morning. Welcome. Come on in. I really appreciate you all coming to help."

"Wouldn't miss it for the world," Lee said. "Where is she? Saul and I can't wait to meet her."

Brandon pointed into the living room. He heard a scream of "Unca Sir-yay" before running feet echoed on the hardwoods, and Casey was wrapped around Sergei's legs. "You came back."

Sergei bent and picked her up as he answered her. "I said I would."

"Not everyone comes back," she said with a very serious look on her face.

"That's true, but you can count on all of us. Ready to meet all these people?"

Casey nodded and turned to look around, her eyes going wide. "That's a lot of people."

Brandon laughed at how serious she was. "That's a lot of family, baby girl, and we're all going to work to make a room suitable for a princess."

"With purple."

Lee stepped forward, holding up the cans of paint he had in each hand. "Lots of purple." He set one can down so he could hold the can closer to her. "See that dot right there? That's what color we're going to paint your room."

"Yay! Purple!"

"Yep. Lots and lots of purple. By the way, I'm your Uncle Lee, and this is my husband, your Uncle Saul."

"I'm Casey. You're big," she said while staring up at Saul.

"Pleased to meet you, Casey. Yep. I ate all my vegetables when I was little, so I grew up big and strong. Do you eat all your vegetable?"

Casey's nose scrunched up as she thought hard about the questions. "I don't like yucky peas, but I like green beans."

Lee leaned in and stage-whispered to Casey. "I don't like peas either. They're squishy." Lee held up his hand for a high five.

"Yeah. Yucky. Squishy. Peas." Casey ended with a blech face, complete with tongue sticking out of her mouth as she slapped Lee's hand.

"You are not helping, Lee." Kirk said as he came up and slapped Lee on the back. "Hi. I'm your Uncle Kirk. My husband, Eric, had to take our girls to soccer practice. They'll be here in about an hour."

"You have little girls like me?" Casey's look was so hopeful that Brandon could hardly stand it.

"Well, they are older than you, but they are looking forward to playing with you."

"Actually," Mama H interrupted from across the room where she had been in conference with Nikolai, "do you think we could borrow them for a few hours?

We are going to take Casey clothes shopping. We could use some expert advice."

"You mean conflicting advice," Kirk said with a grin. "Those two have completely different styles."

"Well, I think it will be good for Casey, and as an added benefit, it gets the little ones out of your hair for a few hours."

"That's true. I have a canopy princess bed in the back of my SUV. Come take a look and see if Casey wants it. She's too big for the toddler bed we had, but Claire had a twin princess bed before we moved into the new house."

Brandon clapped his hands before rubbing them together. "Awesome. Let's get started."

Chapter Nineteen

Brandon closed the door on the last of the helpers. Looking at his watch, he saw that it was already nine p.m. He could hear the boys talking to Nikolai where he was busy folding the freshly washed clothing they had purchased for Casey that day. Stuart and the boys had showed up about an hour ago in time to see the final result.

"Hey, you three, Saul's mama brought supper tonight. There's all sorts of leftovers if you're hungry." Brandon had to step to the side quickly to avoid the stampede.

"Took your life in your own hands there, babe. You should know better than to be between teenage boys and their food, especially when it's cooked by Saul's mama."

Brandon chuckled as he walked over and plopped down on the couch next to Nik and put his hand on Nik's thigh, while glancing over to the other end of the couch at the sleeping three-year-old. "She's out."

"Yep. She's had a busy day. We going to try to put her in her new room tonight or leave her on the couch?"

"We need to check to see if the paint smell is gone yet."

"Yeah. Makes sense," Nik said around a huge yawn as he flopped back on the couch and laid his head on Brandon's shoulder.

"Looks like someone else is tired too."

"Who knew taking an almost-four-year-old shopping was a marathon sport?"

Brandon dropped his head on top of Nik's and laced their fingers together. "I think it was more that she needed everything than anything else. You said you ended up having to go to what? Three stores?"

"Yeah. It was a lot. We have to remember snacks next time, too. I forgot that little ones have to eat more frequently."

"Is that what led to the meltdown at Target?"

"That was certainly part of it. There were a lot of people there, and she saw a shirt she wanted but they didn't have any in her size or bigger. They were all too small for her. It wasn't pretty. We got her some food and some quiet time at the café next door, and she was much better."

Brandon raised the hand not holding Nik's to cover his own jaw-cracking yawn. "We should get her up to use the potty and into some pajamas."

After a few moments where neither one of them moved, Nikolai chuckled. "Look at us—balls of energy on a Saturday night."

"Oh, man. This is sad."

"Come on. You get Casey ready then we can go to bed too." Nikolai stood and gathered all the piles of clothing. "I'll let the boys know where we are, then I'll take these upstairs and put them away and check to see if it's clear enough for her to sleep in there. Lee used the low VOC paint, so it wasn't bad at all when I checked it earlier. I'm thinking she will probably be good to go."

"Yeah. She was very excited to see her room."

"It's definitely girly."

"Oh yeah. Purple and pink and ruffles everywhere."

Brandon scooped Casey up and carried her up the stairs. After stopping at the restroom, he woke her up just enough to get her to go then carried her into her new room. Nik had laid a pair of pajamas on the bed, ready to be put on. Casey opened her eyes and looked around at everything.

"My room," she sighed and flopped her head back on Brandon's shoulder.

"Yep. It's your room. Let's get you into your pajamas, so you can snuggle in your new bed with your animals."

"Okay, Daddy."

Brandon felt his heart lurch. "That's my girl."

Nik came back into the room in time to help Brandon get Casey into her pajamas and Nik pulled back the covers so Brandon could put her in the bed and tuck her in. Nik disappeared from his side to grab Bobo and another of the many stuffed animals that had appeared in the room and tuck them in next to the already-sleeping girl.

Brandon stood and turned on the nightlight next to the bed, before taking Nikolai's hand and leading him out and straight into the master bathroom. "No hanky-panky tonight. I'm wiped."

"Hanky-panky? Really?" Nikolai's giggles had a bit of a hysterical edge to them as he finished undressing.

Brandon's lips twitched, but he worked hard to keep his stern expression. "Yes. We are both way too tired. We'd probably end up hurting ourselves."

Nikolai snorted as he turned on the shower to warm. "I'd be offended if it wasn't so true. We are so lucky we have such great family."

"Oh yeah. It would have taken us days if not weeks to get all this done otherwise." Stepping into the shower, Brandon washed up quickly as they continued their conversation.

"Right? Now, just to take care of all the other things, like childcare and adoption and your mama's funeral."

"The funeral stuff is all done. It's on Tuesday. We didn't want to conflict with all the Memorial Day events. This afternoon, Mama H helped me get in touch with someone to get the tombstone carved, and we called to get the obituary in the paper. I don't know if I told you, but she'll be buried next to my dad, and we're only doing a graveside service. I've already let everyone else know." Brandon rinsed and stepped out of the shower, letting Nik take his place.

"Okay. That works. We bought a nice dress for Casey to wear to it." Nik was equally fast washing up, stepping out of the shower as Brandon was finishing brushing his teeth.

"Oh man. I didn't brush Casey's teeth."

Nikolai wrapped his arms around Brandon from behind. "I think she can survive one night without it. She was exhausted. From what I remember with Sasha and Natasha, it's better to leave her sleeping or we could end up with her bouncing off the walls after her power nap."

Brandon groaned loudly. "I don't think I could handle a bouncing Casey at the moment. I mean, there were so many people helping today, so it went quickly, but my brain is fried."

"I get that. Now, go on. Get into bed. I'll be right behind you."

Brandon dragged his sorry self to the bed and climbed in with a heavy sigh. Snuggling into his pillow and closing his eyes, he was out before Nikolai even made it out of the bathroom.

* * * *

A shaking bed woke him up the next morning. "Is it an earthquake?" he mumbled, still half-to-three-quarters asleep. Giggling was the only response. Opening his eyes, he saw Casey jumping on the bed. She used one hand to shove her curls out of her face.

"Hi, Daddy. Papa Nik said to come wake you up for beckfast. We're having pancakes."

Brandon quirked one eyebrow at her and attempted his most severe parenting expression. "And did he tell you to do it by jumping on the bed?"

Casey's lower lip popped out as she plopped down on her bottom onto the mattress. "No." She then perked up as she added, "But he didn't say not to."

Brandon sat up while laughing. Reaching out, he pulled her across the mattress and into his arms. "Come here, you little lawyer-in-training." He gave her a hug and lightly rubbed his scruffy cheek along her neck, making her giggle.

Nikolai's voice floated up from downstairs. "Ten-minute warning on pancakes. Anyone who wants some needs to get their butts out of bed."

"Pancakes!" Casey's yell next to his ear made him jump.

"You go on back downstairs. Tell Nikolai that I'll be right there."

"Okay, Daddy."

Casey climbed down from the bed and ran out of the door, yelling as soon as she cleared the jamb. "I'm coming, Papa. Daddy be there soon. I waked him up."

Brandon could only shake his head at Casey's volume. "It's too early for this. What the hell time is it anyway?" Glancing at the clock, he was shocked to see that it was almost nine. "I guess I have nothing to complain about." Scrubbing his hands over his face, he stood and grabbed some clothes before heading to the bathroom. Ten minutes later, he made his way downstairs, calling out a greeting to the three boys at the breakfast bar. "Morning, boys."

Good mornings rang out from all three – some clearer than others, depending on the quantity of food in their mouths. They were inhaling pancakes, eggs and bacon at an alarming rate. His wide-eyed gaze met Nikolai's, who chuckled at his expression.

"Don't worry. I saved you some." Reaching into the oven, he pulled out two plates, piled with food. "I waited to eat with you. Casey is almost done," he said, nodding toward the table in the breakfast nook where Casey was sitting. She had syrup and what looked like jam on her face and was grinning at him happily.

Brandon stopped to wet a paper towel so he could clean Casey off once she was done, before sitting down next to her at the table, with Nikolai sitting across from them. Standing back up, he leaned across the table and gave a startled Nikolai a kiss. "Morning, gorgeous."

"Mm-m. Morning."

"What time did you get up?"

"Well, the princess woke me up at six this morning."

"Why didn't you wake me? I could have gotten up with her."

Nikolai waved off his comments. "Not a big deal. I'm a morning person, and you most definitely are not. It's fine."

"Well, thank you for making breakfast. It looks great."

"I helped, Daddy."

Brandon glanced at Nikolai, seeing him pressing his lips together to hide his smile, before turning his attention back to Casey. "Well, thank you too, then. You guys did a great job." He couldn't help smiling back at the huge grin Casey gifted him with for thanking her. "What's on the agenda today?"

"Well, Sasha and Jessie's parents are picking them up at ten-thirty. They had enough of the con yesterday. Mama H has invited all of us over for pizza from their new pizza oven at four today. That's all I know about."

"Jeremy, anything else on your agenda today?"

"Nope. I want to do some homework, so I can spend tomorrow relaxing."

"The school year is almost finished, at least."

"Yep. A few more assignments and it's all done."

"What about you, Sasha? Did you get into the college you wanted?"

"Yep. I got into my top three choices. Now I just have to make a decision."

"That's awesome."

Jessie spoke up. "Sasha has worked really hard to keep his grades outstanding. He's the valedictorian."

"Well, I have to if I want to be a doctor."

"Is that your goal?"

"Yep. I want to be a pediatrician."

Nik shot Sasha a fond look. "It's been Sasha's goal since he was five."

"That's impressive. I think I wanted to be Spider-Man when I was five."

"I still want to be Spider-Man," Jeremy chimed in.

"Why am I not surprised, brother mine? Finish your breakfast then the three of you are on clean-up duty since Nikolai was kind enough to feed us."

The three boys gave nods of agreement before going back to their food. "What do you want to do today, Casey?"

"We go see Mommy?"

Brandon and Nikolai shared a glance then Brandon swallowed hard. This didn't get any easier. "Remember, sweetie. Mommy died and went to heaven. You don't get to see her anymore. We're going to have her funeral on Tuesday, so you can see where she is going to be buried."

"Will she be buried next to your daddy?"

"Yes, baby girl. She's going to be buried next to my daddy, so she won't be alone."

"Okay. That's good." Then in the mercurial mood of a toddler, "Can I go watch cartoons?"

"Sure. Let me wash you up, then we can get you set up with cartoons."

"I'll go turn them on for her, Bran. You eat," Jeremy offered.

"Thanks, Jeremy."

Brandon started washing off Casey's hands and face, then realized one wet paper towel wasn't going to cut it. He picked her up out of her chair and set her on the counter next to the sink. Grabbing a cloth out of the drawer, he wet it and finally managed to get her clean. "There. All done." He kissed her on top of her head then gave her a hug before setting her on the floor. "I hear cartoons in the living room. Maybe you should go see if Jeremy did a good job."

"Hey," Jeremy shouted from the living room, as Casey ran that way. "I resent the implications that I don't know my 'toons, man." Jeremy rejoined them a moment later. "She's all set. I think she might fall back to sleep."

"I'm surprised with all the syrup she just consumed, but she got Nikolai up at six, so it has been almost four hours already, and she's had a lot happen in the last few days."

Nikolai got up and came to take the hand towel from Brandon, where he had been absentmindedly drying his hands. "I think your hands are dry, babe. Come finish eating."

"Oh yeah. Hey, Jeremy, I forgot to tell you that the funeral is Tuesday afternoon. You have a choice—miss the whole school day or go in for a half-day. Funeral isn't until two. We are just doing a private family viewing and a graveside service."

"I have a test in history in the morning, so I would prefer to be picked up after that. I don't want to have to make it up."

"What time would that be?"

"Well lunch starts at 10:40, so any time after that. I think Jessie and Bones wanted to come with me, too."

"Okay. We'll discuss with parents as they pick you guys up. Someone can certainly get you all from school at eleven."

Sasha looked up from where he was putting his plate in the dishwasher. "Actually, I can drive them, so no one has to pick them up."

"Oh, that's right. I forgot seniors can drive."

"Juniors and seniors, Brandon. I can't wait." Jeremy was bouncing with his normal excitement as he was rinsing dishes at the sink. "I can get my junior license next month on my birthday."

"Yeah. That reminds me. We need to get you practicing some more."

"Great." A small hesitation had Brandon looking at his brother more closely. "I was thinking of asking Kirk if I can be an apprentice at his shop, once I turn sixteen."

Brandon paused. "That would actually be a good fit for you and your love of all things cars."

Bounce. Bounce. Bounce. "Then it's okay?"

"Yeah. Give it a shot. I think he will be at the cookout tonight, so maybe you can talk to him then."

"Thanks, Brandon."

"Why? Did you think I would say no?"

Jeremy shrugged. "I just figured you would push me to go to college."

Brandon walked over and gave Jeremy a side hug, leaving his arm around his shoulders. "Dude, I know you don't love school and that you want to be a mechanic more than anything. I would like you to at least take some business classes along with your tech school stuff, but you don't have to follow my path."

Jeremy slumped in apparent relief. Brandon placed a kiss on the side of his head. "Brother of mine, you know you can talk to me about anything. If you were worried, you should have said something. Now, I do still expect you to work hard in school and not just in the classes that interest you, either."

"Yeah. Yeah. Slave driver."

"Yep. That's me." Brandon hugged him again before letting him go. "Maybe when we look at your classes for next year, we can get you to do the business math instead of the calculus, etc. I doubt you'll need calculus in the garage."

Jeremy's face lit up. "Man. Have I ever told you that you're my favorite brother."

"Yeah. Yeah. Once things settle down, we can make an appointment with the guidance counsellor and get things figured out."

"Thanks, Brandon."

"Dude," Sasha whisper-yelled at Jeremy. "Do you think maybe today wasn't the best day to talk to him about that stuff? There's a lot going on."

"I know," Jeremy whisper-yelled back. "It just slipped out."

Jessie sighed loudly. "Well, at least you can stop obsessing about it now."

"Amen to that. I don't think I could do one more role play of him talking to Brandon about it. It was worse than your coming-out speech practice."

"Right?"

Brandon shook his head as he sat back down at the table, sharing a glance with Nikolai as he picked up his fork. Nikolai covered the hand without a fork in it and gave it a squeeze. Nikolai mouthed "good job" to him, and Brandon made a conscious effort to relax his shoulders. The boys finished and left Nikolai and him alone for the first time all morning.

Brandon set down his fork and leaned back in his seat with his glass of juice. "I'm not sure how I missed that he was so stressed out about something."

"Jeremy is one of the happiest kids I know. He didn't want you to know. At least he has a great support system in Sasha and Jessie."

"Why didn't he just talk to me, though?"

"Dude, you're his father figure. He didn't want to disappoint you. You said yourself that your mom and dad both had college degrees. You have a master's and are a bit of a perfectionist. It's very typical teenager behavior."

"Yeah. I guess so." Brandon took another sip of his juice. "Man, this has been the longest two days. Thanks for being here with me."

"Wouldn't want to be anywhere else."

Chapter Twenty

Nik sat back in his chair at work, thankful that he had finally caught up the paperwork from being out the week before. Oh, the garage books had been easy. Kirk had kept up with most of those while he was out. The problem was with his finance clients. Looking through the accounts for all his clients and catching up on all the questions that had come in took a while. After a week, he was back on track.

His cell phone ringing broke him out of his musings. Glancing at the screen, before swiping to answer, he was surprised to see Jeremy calling. "What's up, Jeremy?"

"I think she broke him." Jeremy's whisper had chills going down Nik's back.

"What do you mean 'she broke him'? Who's 'she'?"

"Casey. I guess Brandon had to give her a bath, because she used her washable markers to give herself tattoos like Uncle Kirk. He tried to brush her hair after the bath and now the brush is stuck. He just asked me to watch her for a minute and went upstairs and shut himself in his bedroom."

"Jermy. Help me. The brush stuck." Casey's voice echoed over the phone.

Nikolai chuckled. "Tell Casey I'll be right there. I was leaving in a minute anyway. Let me just tell Kirk that I'm going."

"Okay, hurry."

Nikolai got up and made his way to Kirk's door. "Hey, Kirk. I need to head out. It seems Miss Casey wanted to look like you and used her markers to give herself tattoos today. Jeremy just called me. I guess Brandon and Casey had a rough day."

"I don't know whether to be happy she wants to look like me or appalled, as a sympathetic parent."

"Right? I'll see you Monday."

"Sounds good."

Nikolai made quick work of shutting down his computer and grabbing his things. The ride to Brandon's was accomplished quickly. Pulling into the driveway behind Brandon's car, Nik let himself in through the garage. Casey was sobbing as Jeremy was attempting to get the brush untangled from her hair.

"Here, Jeremy. Let me have her."

"Thank goodness. Brandon is still in his room."

"Okay. Casey, Casey. Come on, girl. It will be okay."

"Daddy said he was going to shave my head. I don't want to die."

"Casey, shaving your head wouldn't kill you."

"Mommy shaved her head and she died."

"Oh, Casey. Your mommy was sick. The medicine made her hair come out. Her head being shaved didn't kill her. We're not going to shave your hair, anyway. You just have super-curly hair, and we need to learn to take care of it. I have an idea. Let me call a friend, who is a hair stylist. She has curly hair like yours. She can help us. Okay?"

Casey nodded as she dropped her head on to Nikolai's shoulder, almost clunking him in the face with the handle of the hairbrush as she did so. Pulling his phone out, he called his friend and after explaining what had happened. She said to bring Casey in.

"Hey, Jeremy!"

Jeremy popped his head out from behind the door of the refrigerator.

"Yeah?"

"Can you come hang with Casey for a minute while I go talk to Brandon real quick?"

"Sure." Jeremy bounded over and took Casey back.

Nikolai ran up the stairs and gently opened the door. Peeking in, he found Brandon asleep crosswise on the bed. Shaking out the blanket, he laid it over Brandon and eased his way out of the room.

"Hey, Jeremy, Brandon is asleep. Tell him where we've gone when he wakes up, please. Come on, Casey. Let's go see my friend and see if she can help us." Casey reached her arms up for Nikolai, and he scooped her up and carried her out to his car.

When they walked into the salon a few minutes later, Dominique came rushing up to greet them. "Boy, what have you done to this doll-baby's hair?" She harrumphed as she saw the stuck hairbrush and gave Nik a death glare. "Really?"

"Hey, I wasn't there. I know better than to use that type of brush on her hair, but I obviously forgot to tell my boyfriend."

"Boyfriend? You've been holding out on me. Tell me all about it. How did you end up with this gorgeous girl?"

"My mommy died, and I live with my brother Brandon now. He's going to be my daddy—and Nik too."

"Well, isn't that great? Nik is going to be a wonderful daddy. I don't know Brandon, but I'm guessing if he's smart enough to date Nik, then he's a great guy too."

Casey nodded, while Nik was quick to respond. "He really is a great guy. I'm very lucky—and you've heard me talk about him. He's the guy that I've always made a fool of myself in front of whenever I was around him."

"Really? You finally wore him down?"

"It wasn't really a case of wearing him down. It turns out he was already raising his brother, who is fifteen. He didn't think he could date until Jeremy graduated."

"Wow. So, you get your man, an adorable little girl and brother all in one go—everything you always wanted."

"Right?"

"Now, let's see what we can do to get this brush out of your cutie's hair."

An hour later Casey was brushless, her hair had been cut to frame her face and her curls were shining with health. "You've done a great job, Dommy."

"She was definitely way overdue for a trim. Now remember… With her hair type, you don't wash it every day. You don't need a lot of the shampoo I just had you buy, either."

"Got it. I'll pass the information on, along with the new brush."

"Good. Now don't be a stranger. We need to get together for a girl's night out soon."

Nik leaned in and kissed Dominique's cheek. "Definitely—and I'll bring her back for a trim in a month or so."

"Eh. You can probably go six weeks…no longer than eight, though."

"Got it."

"Now shoo. I have another client in five minutes."

"I'm just glad you had an opening."

"Me too. It has been great to see you and meet your new baby girl. She's amazing."

Nik smiled so wide his face hurt. "I'm one lucky guy, for sure."

Nik went through the drive-through to grab chicken and potatoes for dinner, before making his way back to Brandon's with Casey talking about "Dom and the bad hairbrush" the whole ride home.

Nik and Casey walked through the front door loaded down with their dinner haul, to be greeted by a scowling Brandon, who was standing at the bottom of the stairs with his arms crossed.

Nik took the food into the kitchen and set it on the counter as Casey went running to Brandon. "Look, Daddy. Look how pretty my hair is—and the bad brush is gone. Dom said we had to use this brush." She waved the new brush around in the air in front of him.

Brandon looked at Casey and gave her a mostly genuine smile. "That's nice. Your hair does look amazing, sweetie. Why don't you take your new brush upstairs to your bathroom then can you go to your room and play for a few minutes while I talk to Nik?"

"Okay, Daddy." Casey ran up the stairs yelling for Jeremy. "Jer-my! Jer-my! Look at my hair."

Brandon turned his gaze to Nik, and Nik took a step back at the anger in his expression. "What's wrong?"

"What's wrong? You take Casey without my permission and get her hair cut by some stranger I haven't met?"

"Without your *permission*? You were asleep, and the child had a brush stuck in her hair. My friend Dom had an opening at her salon, and I took Casey to get some help. I know nothing about mixed-race hair or how to take care of Casey's curls. As my friend Dominique is Black, I figured she would be able to help—and she did!"

"I'm not saying her hair doesn't look great. It does, but you did it without checking with me!"

"I thought we were partners. Why would I need to get your permission for a haircut—or was that just talk?"

"And I thought you were going to adopt Casey with me?"

"What?" Nikolai was totally confused.

"I got a call from my lawyer while you were gone," Brandon all but snarled. "He told me how you took your name off the adoption petition. What? Is adoption too much commitment? Too serious for you?"

"What are you talking about?"

"I'm talking about *you* flitting around in your fancy clothes like a little butterfly with no responsibility. You have a doctorate in finance, for goodness sake, but you work at a garage, and now you can't even follow through on the adoption. Are you even planning on sticking around?"

Nik flinched at Brandon's comments, automatically shrinking from his anger, before his own anger came rushing through. "First of all, not that you've ever asked, but I am only staying at the garage until the end of summer. In September, I start training with the CFO of Sergei's company. Mr. Sorenson retires at the end of the year. I am taking over as the CFO upon his retirement." Nikolai raised a finger to stop Brandon when he went to interrupt.

"In the meantime, I am helping out a friend who needed someone to work the front desk at his shop, and I needed a place to stay. Kirk is looking for my replacement now, since I told him I would be moving in with you. In addition to that, I am working pro bono with people getting out of prison through an outreach program, as well as a few low-income families to help them learn budgeting, etc. and hopefully put them on a good financial path. I have also been busy starting a relationship with you. Although, it doesn't appear that will be taking up too much more of my time."

Nikolai's entire body was now shaking with his anger. "As far as the adoption, your lawyer told me this morning that if we added my name to the petition, it would drag out the adoption because first of all, we are not married and secondly, my name isn't on the guardianship paperwork. I told him that Casey's security came first, so to drop my name from the petition for now and that I would submit adoption paperwork later, after we got married."

Brandon slumped, like a puppet with its strings cut. "Oh."

"Yeah, '*oh*'. How dare you? If this is really what you think of me, why did you even ask me to move in?" Nikolai held up his hand when Brandon took a step toward him. "Never mind. I don't want to know. Dinner is on the counter along with the new shampoo for Casey. You only have to wash her hair at most every other day. We were drying the hell out of it. Now, let me flit myself out of your presence."

Nikolai strode toward the door, avoiding Brandon's outstretched hand. "Nik. Wait! I'm sorry."

Nikolai spun around when he reached the door and glared at Brandon. "Whatever. I have worked too hard to be comfortable in my own skin to have you criticize every part of me. Good luck with *your* daughter. I'll see you around."

Nik couldn't look at the devastation on Brandon's face any longer, nor could he stand there looking at Brandon while his heart was breaking. He was five seconds away from losing it, so he spun back to the door and yanked it open, making sure to slam it behind him. He managed to hold it together long enough to get in his car and drive down the street before he had to pull over and lose it.

He didn't know how long he sat there, but eventually the storm passed and he was able to clean up his face and blow his nose with napkins from the glove compartment. *Good thing I'm not wearing makeup today.* The garage was still open, so Nikolai snuck through the outside door, so he wouldn't run into anyone. His phone started ringing for the third time as he let himself in the door. Glancing at the screen, he saw that Brandon was calling him, but since he wasn't ready to talk to Brandon yet, he sent it to voicemail before going to turn off his phone entirely. It rang in his hand as he was about to swipe to complete the action. To his surprise, his academic advisor's name was on the screen. He hurriedly clicked 'accept'.

"Good evening, sir."

"Good evening, Nikolai. I have a great opportunity for you..."

Nik took a deep breathe to center himself. "I'm listening…"

Chapter Twenty-One

The door slammed behind Nik. Brandon shook himself and hurried to it, getting it open in time to see Nik back out of the driveway.

Jeremy's voice coming from behind him made him jump. "You certainly wonked that up, bro."

Brandon scrubbed his face with both hands. "I know. I need to call him. Where's Casey?"

"She's playing in her room."

"Okay, good." Brandon pulled his phone out of his pocket and dialed Nik's number, not surprised when it rang four times before eventually going to voicemail. "Hey, Nik. I'm sorry. I was way out of line. Please call me or better yet come back. Please." Brandon hung up the phone and knocked the upper corner of it against his forehead, thinking hard. He dialed Nik's number again. "I'm so sorry. It's just you seem to do it all right, and I can't seem to do anything right with Casey. I got a damn hairbrush stuck in her hair. She was crying and it was my fault. You swept in and fixed it when I couldn't. I'm used to being the one to fix things, but this is all on me. I'm the one…" Brandon paused to take a deep breath then hung up the phone when he realized he was losing it. He sank to the bottom step of the stairs and simply let go.

Jeremy's arms came around him, and Brandon tried to pull himself back together. "I've got you, Brandon. We've got this. We're all a team. Nik will forgive you. Shh. It's okay."

Brandon distantly heard Jeremy's words, as if through cotton wool. "What am I going to do if he won't?"

"He will. Nik loves you."

"Yeah?"

"Yeah. He waited a long time for you. I doubt he will give up after one argument."

"I hope you're right."

"I *know* I'm right. Now why don't you go take a shower? You'll feel better for it, I'm sure, and really, you stink. I can watch Casey."

Brandon stood and gave his brother a hug. "You're right. I'll do that. Thanks, Jeremy." Brandon wearily trudged up the stairs. Making it to his bedroom, he closed the door behind him and stripped off his clothes on his trek to the bathroom, letting them fall wherever along the way.

He turned on the water to its hottest setting, climbed in and started scrubbing every part of his body, starting with his hair. When he finished, he stood under the spray and let the strong water pressure beat on his tense muscles. Eventually, the water started to cool, so he turned off the water and reached for his towel, feeling exhausted emotionally and physically.

After wrapping the towel around his waist, Brandon picked his phone up off the counter and tried dialing

Nik again. This time it immediately went to voice mail. "Nik. I know I screwed up. I didn't mean it. You work harder than anyone I know and I'm a mess, but don't leave me. I swear I'm worth it. I love you." Brandon hung up then dragged his sorry ass to bed, still clutching his phone and willing it to ring. Once there, he pulled the covers up and over his head, closing his eyes with a sigh.

He woke up who knew how long later and immediately searched for his phone. He finally found it under his pillow. Looking at the screen, he realized he had fallen asleep for four hours and it was now ten o'clock at night. He also saw he had missed a call and voicemail from Nik. He clicked the button to listen to the voicemail as he sat up and put the phone to his ear.

"Hi. Um. I got your voicemails. I love you too. You know I do – and I can understand why hearing that I said I wasn't going to adopt Casey with you would upset you." Pause and a deep breath. "It's not okay that you yelled at me like that, though. It's not. I deserve better. I know these aren't normal times, and we've both been on a bit of a rollercoaster for the last month. Maybe we should take a step back and reevaluate. I've been invited to present a paper I wrote at a huge conference in Las Vegas this week, as they've had someone cancel. It's a huge honor. I guess that's all I have to say right now. We can talk when I get back."

Brandon listened to the voicemail message three times before he pressed the button to try to call Nik. It, of course, went to voicemail. "Hi, Nik. I understand. Good luck at your conference. I wish you nothing but good things. Goodbye." If the last was said on a sob, Brandon wasn't ever going to admit it.

He got up and went to check on Casey. She was asleep in her bed, snuggled up with her monkey. He found Jeremy in the living room, playing his war game online with his friends. Jeremy had his headset on and was trying to be quiet as he talked into the microphone. Brandon gave him a wave as he went to kitchen to get something to eat. He wasn't hungry, but he couldn't remember when he'd last eaten anything. He needed to stay healthy for his family.

Jeremy came into the kitchen a moment later, his gaze filled with concern. "You doing okay?"

"Yep."

Jeremy scoffed. "Lies. You look like crap."

"Yeah well, Nik just broke up with me."

"What? No way."

"Yes...way."

"Did he say that?"

"Not exactly."

When Brandon didn't say anything else, Jeremy prodded him. "What did he say *exactly*?"

"He said we needed to take a step back and reevaluate. He will be gone to a conference and maybe we could talk when he gets back."

"That doesn't mean he wants to break up with you. Dude, don't give up like that."

"I don't have the energy right now, Jeremy. We have things we need to do. I go back to work on Monday. You have your last week of school. Casey starts at her new preschool, and I may need to add looking for a new job to my list."

"What? Why?"

"Well, Nik is going to be the new CFO for Sergei, which means I will be working with him a lot. If we've broken up, I don't think I'll be able to handle that."

"You haven't broken up. You can't really believe that."

Brandon knew his expression wasn't pleasant, even without Jeremy jerking back. He was heartbroken, and there was no hiding that at the moment.

"I'm not enough for anyone," Brandon whispered. "I wasn't enough for Mom to stay sober. I'm not enough for Nik. He deserves better, and so do you and Casey — but I'm all you've got."

"What? Brandon, you're the best. You take care of everyone. You take care of Sergei and his company. He couldn't do it without you. He told me so. As for me, I am so thankful every day that you stepped up and got custody of me. You make me feel safe, and I know I can count on you. Always. Casey adores you. You aren't going to be perfect. No parent is. No boyfriend is. Don't give up."

Brandon pulled Jeremy into his arms. "Thanks for the pep talk, Jeremy. I appreciate it."

"You know, you got me into counseling with Dr. Anders. Maybe you should go too."

Brandon thought for a long moment. "You're right. Mrs. Robinson said something similar. It would probably be a good idea for all of us. This has been a lot. I'll call and make the appointment on Monday."

"Okay. Now, eat something then go back to bed. You look like crap."

Brandon pulled up a smile from somewhere. "Thanks."

"Anytime. I don't say it a lot, but I love you."

"Love you, too."

Jeremy gave him one more hug before snagging a soda from the refrigerator and going back to the living room. Brandon grabbed some leftover pizza from dinner the night before, heated it and sat down at the breakfast bar to eat. He pulled his laptop closer to him, remembering that Dr. Anders had an online appointment request system. After lucking into an obvious cancellation slot for the next afternoon, he pulled up the job search engine to check to see what was out there.

* * * *

Brandon was setting down Casey's plate for breakfast the next morning, when the doorbell started ringing. It rang again, before Brandon had even cleared the kitchen and again as he was walking toward the door. "I'm coming. Be patient." He swung the door open on an irate Sergei. "What?"

Sergei pushed his way past Brandon and into the living room. "What's this I hear that you're looking for another job?"

"What?" Brandon groaned. "Jeremy...I'm not looking, looking. I was seeing what was out there in case..." Brandon trailed off, not knowing how to continue that sentence.

"No." Sergei pointed a finger at Brandon. "You cannot quit. I won't allow it."

Brandon couldn't help but smirk at Sergei as he shook his head. "I don't want to quit, but Nik said he is going to be the CFO. I don't want to make him uncomfortable."

"And why would it make him uncomfortable to work with his boyfriend?"

"He broke up with me last night. I got upset over something stupid and yelled at him. He left, refused to pick up any of my calls then left me a voicemail."

"I talked to Nik this morning. I loaned him the private jet for his flight to Las Vegas. He didn't mention anything about you guys breaking up. What did he say *exactly*?"

"He said we needed to take a step back and reevaluate." Brandon held up a finger to stop Sergei from speaking. "I think it's pretty clear, especially as he never answered any of my phone calls. Anyway, he can do better, find someone without all the baggage I have. He has his whole life ahead of him."

"*Fignya*! *Nyet*. No."

"You can't call bullshit on this. It has nothing to do with you."

"It does if you are even thinking of quitting." Sergei pulled out his phone and dialed. "Nikolai." That was the only word Brandon followed since he switched to rapid-fire Russian. Brandon knew some of Sergei's most used phrases like *fignya* or bullshit, but he really needed to work on learning the language when he had time. Brandon scoffed to himself. *If it's even necessary anymore*. He turned around and headed back to the kitchen to see what Casey was doing.

"Hey, sweetie." Brandon kissed her head as he went by. "Pancakes good?" Casey nodded with chipmunk cheeks full of pancake. "Smaller bites, Case. You're going to choke. No one is going to take your food from you. Okay?"

Casey nodded again and started humming as she chewed.

Jeremy joined them in the kitchen, still wearing his pajamas and yawning as he came in. "What's Sergei doing here?"

"You tell me. Somehow he heard I was considering looking for another job." Brandon quirked an eyebrow at Jeremy. "I wonder who he could have heard that from?"

Jeremy looked embarrassed. "Sorry. I said something to the guys last night about what was going on. Sasha must have said something to Sergei."

"No." Sergei's voice made them all jump. "Sasha told Mama. Mama called me. Now I have called Nikolai. Here! He wishes to speak to you."

Brandon took the phone like it was a bomb and tentatively raised it to his ear. "Hello?"

Chapter Twenty-Two

Nikolai had just finished listening to Brandon's voicemail message, wondering at the air of defeat in Brandon's tone when the phone rang in his hand with Sergei's ringtone. He answered distractedly. "Hello, Sergei. Thanks for letting me borrow the company jet."

"Nikolai." It took Nik a moment to follow the epic rant Sergei was raining down on him in Russian.

"Wait. Wait. I didn't break up with Brandon."

"He thinks you did. He said you needed to take a step back and reevaluate. Now he is looking for another job."

"He yelled at me."

"Oh, boo-hoo. In the last few months, the man has come clean to all of us about his home life, gotten a boyfriend, lost his mother and gained custody of a four-year-old he didn't even know existed. Cut the man some damn slack. Did he hit you? Did he call you a rat bastard whore?"

"No!" Nik yelled back, appalled Sergei would even say such a thing. "He said I couldn't flit through life."

"And? Did you share with him what your plans for life were?"

"Well, no. We haven't had a chance to discuss any of it. As you said, there's been a lot going on."

"So…you told a man who is floundering because he has so much on his plate at the moment that you needed to take a step back and reevaluate—a man who has been let down and abandoned by every member of his family who should have been looking out for him, a man who has had to shoulder way more responsibility than he should have at a very, young age. That's the man you told you needed to step back and reevaluate. How did you think he would take that?"

"Oh." Nikolai was beginning to feel like he might have overreacted.

"Yeah, '*oh*'. According to what Jeremy told Sasha, Brandon is partly struggling because he's not doing things perfectly and thinks you are much better at being Casey's parent than him."

"That's not true. Brandon is fantastic with her. He's her safe place, the one she goes to whenever she is scared or hurt or hungry. I'm the one she comes to when she wants to play."

"Sounds to me like you guys need to work on your communication. I mean, you should have picked up the phone and called Brandon about dropping your name from the custody thing—immediately, at the very least. That is not a nice thing to get surprised with by your lawyer."

"Yeah." The word came out quiet and small, exactly how he was feeling.

Sergei exhaled a loud sound of disappointment. "I'm at Brandon's house now. Would you like to talk to him?"

"*Da.*"

He heard Sergei speaking then a hesitant "Hello."

"Baby, I didn't break up with you. I had my feelings hurt, but I wasn't breaking up with you."

Brandon gasped. "You weren't?"

"No," Nikolai made his voice as firm as possible. "I know I'm a bit of a drama queen, but don't even think for a minute I am letting you go. I love you. You're stuck with me, but I do think Sergei is right, and we need to work on our communication."

"Yeah. I should have gotten your side of the story before jumping down your throat about not adopting Casey."

"And as Sergei just told me, I should have called you as soon as I got off the phone with the lawyer. That wasn't a decision that should have waited until I saw you to tell you about it, especially since I knew the lawyer was calling you later. I'm sorry I upset you, and for the record, you are doing a great job with Casey."

"Except for her hair." Nikolai was happy to hear Brandon's usual dry humor coming through.

"Yeah, well, none of us were doing her hair right, so you weren't alone in that."

"You weren't the one to get a hairbrush stuck in it. Not my finest moment, for sure. Listen... I made an appointment for this afternoon to speak to the counsellor Jeremy and I saw when he first came to live with me. I'm going to get Casey in to see someone as well."

"Okay. That sounds like a great idea."

"Um-m. She also does couple's therapy. Would you be willing to do something like that with me?" Brandon continued before Nikolai could answer him. "You don't have to, but I thought it wouldn't hurt."

"Brandon, stop. Yes, I will do couple's therapy with you. I mean, we're new, but there is a lot, I mean a whole lot, of stuff going on, and I want to give us our best chance."

"Thank you."

"No, thank you for thinking I'm worth it."

"You so are. Just for future, please don't walk away from me then not communicate. I would prefer you didn't leave when we're fighting, but if you need some space, I at least need a text message telling me where you are. It killed me last night when you wouldn't answer the phone. You were so upset when you left, and I was worried you were in an accident or something. I won't come where you are, but I just need to know that you're okay."

Nikolai swallowed hard. "That sounds reasonable. I didn't mean to hurt you like that."

"I know. It's just that my dad left for work one day and didn't come back. I have to know where my people are, especially before I go to bed at night."

"Completely understandable and you are definitely one of my people too, so the same rules apply."

"Fair enough. Now, why do you suddenly have to present a paper in Vegas?"

"I received a phone call from my advisor. One of the presenters at the conference had to pull out, because they got appendicitis—like ignored the pain until it ruptured appendicitis. He is very ill in the hospital. My advisor is on the conference committee and recommended one of my papers for presentation as a replacement."

"That is a fantastic honor. How are you feeling about it?"

"A little nervous, if I'm honest. Presentations are not my favorite thing, and this will be presenting to a bunch of professionals in my own field."

"Well, your advisor obviously has faith in you. I'm sure you'll do a great job. Sorry I can't be there to support you, but I'm proud of you."

"Oh. Thank you. That means a lot."

The pilot's voice came over the speaker, telling him they were getting ready to go and for him to shut down any devices.

"Hey, I've got to go. I'll call when I land in Vegas, okay?"

"Yep. I'll look forward to your call. Love you."

"Love you too."

Nikolai put his things away then took a white-knuckled grip of the armrests. He really didn't enjoy flying too much. Although, flying in a private jet was certainly nicer than flying commercial, even first class. Nik stood up once they were at cruising altitude and shook out his hands as he made his way to the galley to grab something to eat. The door to the front cabin was open when he got there, so he yelled into the pilot and co-pilot.

"Hey, Brian, Stan. Did either of you want something to eat? I see nice sandwiches in the fridge here."

The two men exchanged glances before the captain spoke up, "You go first, Stan. Should be pretty smooth sailing. I had a huge breakfast with my sister right before I came to the airport, so I'm nowhere near hungry yet."

"Well, I didn't have time to eat, so I will certainly take you up on that offer. I am so thankful that Sergei keeps the plane galley well stocked."

"Me too. I'm starving. I haven't eaten since lunchtime yesterday."

Stan spoke through a mouthful of sandwich. "Really?"

"Manners, dude. Gross." Nikolai shrugged his shoulders. "Yeah. Got into an argument with my boyfriend, so I wasn't hungry."

"Oh. That's not cool. Was he a total jerk?"

"He was a bit of a jerk, but I was actually worse. I stormed out like a complete diva and left him to worry if I was okay. I refused to answer any of his calls, and he thought we'd broken up." Nikolai bit into his own sandwich with a groan. *So good.*

Stan winced. "Yeah, that's a big no-no. You at least need to let the other person know you're safe."

Nikolai shrugged again and finished chewing before he responded. "Well, I didn't know. This is my first relationship. Who knew there were so many rules?"

Stan clapped Nikolai on the shoulder. "You'll get there. Just keep working at it."

"That's the plan. I love him. I need to figure it out quickly, though, because I don't want to lose him."

"If he's smart, he'll never let you go."

"That's the goal." Nikolai threw his trash away then grabbed a drink from the refrigerator before making his way back to his seat. The trip flew by as Nikolai used his time on the plane to go over his notes and slides for his presentation. He wasn't actually speaking until Monday morning, but he wanted to be as prepared as possible. His advisor was already there and wanted to get together for lunch the next day. He had offered to look over the presentation afterward to see if there were any areas for improvement. It had been an offer Nikolai was very quick to accept.

He had just finished the last page when Brian came back over the speakers. "Nik, we're getting ready for our descent into Vegas. Please pack up any electronics."

Nikolai quickly put all his things away and made sure his seatbelt was secure, before assuming his position holding tightly to the armrests. It was a useless exercise he knew but one that helped keep him calm. He let out the breath he had been holding when the wheels touched the ground, and it wasn't long before the plane was coming to a stop next to a hanger.

Nikolai collected his belongings and made his way to the exit, where Stan was holding out his garment bag with his suits in it. "We'll be ready to go as soon as you give the word. Sergei said he didn't need us this week, so we can just hang out here in Vegas until you are ready."

"Sounds great. Do you guys have a hotel room yet?"

"Yep. Sergei booked us a suite next to yours."

Nikolai chuckled. "Did he ask you guys to keep an eye on me?"

Brian laughed from behind Stan as Stan winced. "He may have."

"I figured. Now, do what you guys need to do. Looks like the car Sergei booked us is over there. We can all ride together to the hotel."

"Sounds like a plan," Stan said. "We don't have too much to do. We will meet you at the car in a few minutes."

The next few days were a whirlwind of meeting and talking to people. His presentation was well received, and he had been approached with three different job offers, which he'd declined. The whole time, he'd just wanted to go home. He had Facetimed Brandon

Sunday afternoon for him, evening for Brandon, and they'd spent a couple of hours talking about everything — plans and dreams, things they should have already been talking about, but hadn't had the time. Emotionally, he felt closer to Brandon than ever.

Currently he was looking at a very happy but exhausted little girl, after her first day at her new preschool.

"I love my new teacher. Ms. Williams is so funny and knows the best songs." Casey dissolved into giggles for a moment.

"Oh yeah? What did she sing?"

"We sang a song about making a funny face. We had to move our eyes and wiggle our nose." She looked sad for a moment. "I can't wink."

"Well, we can practice when I get home. How does that sound?"

Casey brightened immediately. "Yeah. Let's do that. When do you come home? I miss you."

"I'll be home Wednesday night. Two more sleeps."

"Yay! Brandon, Nikolai will be home in two more sleeps."

"I heard, sweetie." Brandon came into the frame and pulled Casey onto his lap so Nikolai could see both of them. "Say good night then go to the kitchen. Jeremy has a snack for you."

"Bye, Papa. I love you. See you soon."

"Love you too. I'll talk to you tomorrow night, okay?"

"Okie dokie. I've got to hurry, or Jeremy will eat my snack." She wiggled to be let go. Jeremy's voice came over the speaker.

"I ate your snack one time, when I thought you were done. *One* time."

Casey's giggle echoed along with the sound of her running feet. Nikolai grinned at Brandon.

"Sounds like she had a great first day."

"Yeah. She apparently has a new best friend named Zach, too."

"I'm so sorry I missed the whole 'taking her to her first day and meeting the teacher thing'. I'm going with you to take her for her first day of kindergarten, though — no matter what."

"Well, that's not for a year. Her birthday is in July. She'll only be four."

"That's good, right?"

"Yep. She does make the cut-off for next year, even with the year-round schools. I called the school and talked to them. Basically, we have a year of preschool first."

"Okay. Makes sense."

"You come home Wednesday?"

"Yeah. The conference finishes up at lunchtime on Wednesday. Brian, Stan and I plan to fly out directly after. I should hopefully be back to Raleigh by sometime after dinner, but hopefully before Casey's bedtime."

There was a slight pause before Brandon hesitantly spoke again. "Are you coming to the house or your apartment?"

"I'll definitely come to the house. I miss all of you so much."

Brandon relaxed back into his seat on the couch. "We miss you too. So much. Too bad you weren't coming back a little earlier though, for a lot of reasons. Remember that we meet with the architect at the building for the new youth center Wednesday morning, now that the purchase has gone through."

"Oh man, I forgot about that completely."

"Well, there's been a lot going on. I have all of our notes and this is the initial meeting, so there's time to add things if I forget anything."

"What time is the meeting?"

"It's at ten o'clock."

"Okay. Let me check the itinerary and see if I need to stay until Wednesday. There's a speaker I'm excited to hear at Tuesday night's dinner, but maybe I can leave right after that. I really want to be there for all the steps in this project."

"I know you do, babe. That's why I brought it up."

"Thank you." Nikolai took a moment to simply stare at his boyfriend.

"What?"

"I'm lucky to have you — and I miss you."

"I miss you too."

Nikolai swallowed hard. "Promise me we'll work hard to move forward."

"I promise, babe. I don't want to lose you. You're the love of my life."

"Well, that's convenient, because you're the love of mine."

"That *is* convenient. Listen... I need to go get the kiddo to bed. Can I call you a bit later?"

"I'm meeting Brian and Stan for dinner here in a few minutes. Maybe a couple of hours? I don't want you to stay up too late. I know it's your first week back to work after being off for these last two weeks. You look exhausted."

Brandon's sudden yawn seemed to surprise him. "Yeah. I've been on the run so much today that I didn't realize how tired I was until you mentioned it."

"I know, love. This time difference sucks. We can talk again tomorrow. You need to get some rest."

Another jaw-cracking yawn came from Brandon. "Yeah. I guess you're right. Same time tomorrow?"

"Sounds good. Texts are always welcome, though."

"You got it. I'll keep you posted on how the day goes. Love you."

"Love you too. Sleep well." Brandon kissed his fingers and pressed them to the screen. Nikolai mirrored the motion, letting his fingers linger and enjoying the look of adoration in Brandon's eyes. "See you soon."

The screen went blank, and Nikolai sat back, closing his eyes for a moment to savor the feeling of being part of something bigger than himself. He had a family who adored him. He had a job waiting for him that he was going to love. Above all else, he had Brandon. He'd wanted him for so long, and he'd almost blown it by having a temper tantrum. He needed to be more diligent. Knocking at the door interrupted his introspection.

"Hey, Brian. Hi, Stan. You guys ready to eat?"

"Yep."

"Listen... I just got off the phone with Brandon. I forgot I had a meeting at ten Wednesday morning in Raleigh. Is there any way we could leave after the dinner and guest speaker on Tuesday night?"

"Oh yeah. That's definitely doable. Stan and I can sleep tomorrow then we'll head over to the hangar and get everything ready. What time do you think you will be done?"

"Dinner is scheduled from six to eight with the speaker at seven. I would skip it if it wasn't a someone I really want to hear. She's my idol and a well-known expert in the field. That's a long way of saying I can probably be at the airport by nine."

"Great. We'll file the flight plan for ten to give you some wiggle room."

"Fantastic."

Chapter Twenty-Three

Brandon strolled around the building with Sergei as they waited for the architect to show up.

"Is Nikolai going to make it for the meeting, Brandon?"

"Not sure. I haven't heard from him since he sent a text when they were finally getting ready to take off last night — or I guess it was early this morning. They had a sensor go bad that had to be replaced before they could get in the air. He was not happy."

"Well, I hope he got some sleep on the plane."

A sudden shout made them both jump. "Barinov!"

Coming around the corner into the reception area, Brandon was surprised to see the former CEO of Trinity Corporation standing there.

"Sanderson. What are you doing here?"

"You! You've ruined me! It's all your fault!"

"No, it is yours for being such a horrible person. Did you think I would just let you say ugly things about my mother and others? Give money to groups that harm people? That is not how a leader acts." Sergei flicked his wrist out in a crisp movement to see past his cuff and glance at his watch. "I have an appointment in a few minutes, so I really don't have time to talk to you right now. How did you know I was here, anyway?"

"I saw you come into the building and I followed you. How could you take my company from me?"

"Well, let's see. I spent a lot of money and bought up enough stock to be a majority shareholder. I then fired you. What about that is not clear?"

"Um, Sergei," Brandon said quietly out of the side of his mouth. "Maybe dial it back just a little. The man looks a little unhinged." He truly did. Usually the man was dressed impeccably, but today his suit was a wrinkled mess and he looked like he had been repeatedly running his hands through his hair, as there were strands sticking straight up.

Reaching into his jacket pocket, Sanderson pulled out a gun and aimed it at Sergei. "You will call an emergency board meeting and tell them you made a mistake, and you will get them to rehire me."

Brandon gasped, not knowing what to say, while Sergei put his hands up in a placating manner. "That's not how it works, Sanderson, but we can talk about it. Put the gun down."

He started waving the gun around erratically as he ranted. "You ruined me. I have no job, and my wife left me! The company was everything to me! Everything will be okay if you give me my job back now – or I can shoot you. Your choice."

Sergei reached into his pocket and pulled out his phone. "Okay. Calm down. Let me call and get everyone in for a meeting." He dialed 9-1-1 and put his phone to his ear. Brandon could only hear Sergei's side of the conversation, but the man deserved an Oscar for his performance.

"Oh. Hello. This is Sergei Barinov. It seems Mr. Sanderson is most upset about me firing him from his position as CEO at Trinity Corporation. He has confronted me with a gun at a building I've purchased at two-two-seven Fayetteville Street. He is demanding I call an emergency board meeting to reinstate him. Could you please pull everyone together for say an hour?" Pause. "Yes, that would be wonderful, if you could. As soon as possible." Brandon watched as Sergei pretended to hang up the phone but left it on so the dispatcher could hear what was going on.

"Are they going to meet?"

"Yes. You heard me. Everything is being arranged now."

Mr. Sanderson started pacing back and forth in front of the door, becoming more and more agitated. He spun to face them again. "Where? I didn't hear you say where the meeting is going to be."

Brandon watched as a brief look of panic crossed Sergei's face, before his expression cleared. "Ah. You missed my assistant's side of the conversation. It will be in our corporate office, of course."

"You're lying!"

As Sanderson started to raise the gun, to Brandon's horror, Nikolai stepped up from behind him and did some kind of hammer chop on Sanderson's gun hand. The surprise and force of the move made Sanderson drop the gun. Nikolai then jumped on Sanderson's back and put him in a choke hold while pulling him backward. They both landed with a crash on the floor.

Brandon scrambled to grab the gun before Sanderson could get it again, but he needn't have worried. When he looked back, Nikolai had Sanderson completely immobilized by wrapping his legs around Sanderson's in some sort of submission hold that Sanderson couldn't seem to shake. The man screamed in frustration before collapsing in a sobbing heap.

"Nikolai!"

"Hi, babe. Made it in time for the meeting."

"What? I don't care about the stupid meeting," Brandon yelled, his voice echoing in the open space. "Are you okay?"

Nikolai looked offended. "Of course."

The police arrived in force at that moment, and they were surrounded by lots of men and women in uniform. Sergei was speaking into his phone before hanging it up and putting it back into his jacket pocket. "Did you see that?"

"What?"

"Nikolai taking that guy down."

"Yeah, that was really impressive. I mean I know he has a black belt, but that was ninja-level stuff there. I didn't see how he immobilized him, though—just the takedown."

A cop came to speak to them, and Brandon handed off Sanderson's gun to him. When Nikolai joined them a moment later, Brandon didn't care who was there. He yanked Nikolai into his arms, feeling like he could finally breathe again after he had him in his arms. "You scared the crap out of me."

"Me? You were the one being held at gunpoint."

"Technically that was me, Nikolai," Sergei offered.

Nikolai lifted his head from where he was pressed to Brandon's chest to roll his eyes at Sergei. "Yeah. Yeah. What was with antagonizing the crazy man?"

"You heard that?"

"Yes. I got here a few minutes ago and really needed the restroom. I was going to text once I was done and find out where you guys were. I walked out to this insanity." Nikolai waved his hand in the general direction of the lobby.

"Whatever. I was just telling Brandon how impressive you were taking Sanderson down. Sadly, Brandon missed the end of the move while he was getting the gun."

"You did?"

"Yeah. Sergei was really excited by it, though."

Nikolai smirked at him and waggled his eyebrows, before going up on tiptoe to whisper in his ear. "I can show you what I did and put you in a submission hold later. Would you like that?" Nikolai licked Brandon's ear before nibbling the lobe and letting it go. "You, completely at my mercy?"

Brandon's shudder made Nikolai's grin widen. "Stop that. We still have to get through the statements with the police and the meeting with the architect. I don't want to do either of those things with a hard-on."

Nikolai's grin went even more wicked. "Something for you to look forward to later, then."

Brandon couldn't help the raspiness of his voice as he responded, "Promise?"

"Oh yeah. Count on it." Nik leaned in and gave him a brief kiss, sticking just the tip of his tongue between Brandon's lips before pulling away.

Brandon reached for him, ready to pull him close again, but Nikolai danced just out of reach. The cop clearing his throat reminded Brandon that they weren't alone. "Sorry. What do you need from us?"

* * * *

Way too many hours later, Brandon pulled into his driveway. He had a few minutes before everyone would be home. Nikolai was surprising Casey by picking her up from school, and Jeremy was being dropped off by Sasha in an hour after play practice. Dragging himself out of the car, he went in and up the stairs to the master bathroom. After putting his suit in the bag for dry cleaning, he started the shower and stepped in to try to get the terror sweat off his body.

When he had scrubbed three times, he finally felt clean enough to get out of the shower. Stepping out of the bathroom, he grabbed clothes and threw them on before collapsing into the chair in the corner of the bedroom. The shaking was not a surprise. He was kind of impressed that he'd held it together as long as he had, if he were being honest with himself. The sob *was* a surprise, and he lost it completely. He jerked when arms came around him but couldn't pull himself together enough to do anything. He slumped farther into Nikolai's arms when he spoke, and Brandon realized who it was holding him.

"Sh-h, babe. I've got you."

All Brandon could do was nod his head. Speaking was beyond him at this point. Nikolai continued to rock and hold him, rubbing his back and trying to soothe him. The storm finally passed, and they were quiet for a moment before Nikolai spoke. "We have had a really crappy week, Brandon."

Brandon snorted out a laugh. "It has certainly not been one of our better ones. That's for sure. How are you so calm?"

Nikolai inhaled deeply. "I've had time to get recentered and realize what I want. That's you, in case you were wondering." He reached over to the bedside table and grabbed a couple of tissues out of the box located there and used them to gently clean Brandon's face. "Now, the thing today? I've trained my whole life for a moment like that." Nikolai waggled his eyebrows at Brandon. "I got to be a hero. How cool is that?"

Brandon tried to give Nikolai his sternest expression. "Not cool at all. You scared me to death. I can't lose you." Brandon tightened his arms around Nikolai and dropped his head onto his shoulder. "I can't."

Nikolai rubbed his hand up and down Brandon's back. "I know, babe. I know. You won't lose me. You're stuck with me forever. Even if I die before you in our old, old age, I will come back and haunt your ass until you join me."

Brandon raised his head to glare at Nikolai, trying not to laugh. "You are so not right. Do you know that?"

"Made you laugh, though. You need to focus on the positives. No one got hurt and Sanderson will get the help he needs. I got a call from a friend of mine who is a cop on the way to pick up Casey. He wanted to make sure I was okay. He told me that Sanderson's wife left him because he has a pretty hardcore cocaine habit and has gone through most of their savings. Losing his job was the last straw for her."

"That's sad. I mean, I know what living with an addict looks like. It's exhausting."

"Yep. I know, but Jeremy and Casey are lucky to have you in their corner."

"And you."

"Yep. I'm not going anywhere."

Brandon rolled his eyes. "And you'll haunt my ass if you die before me."

"Now you've got it." Nikolai stood up and ran his hand through Brandon's hair. "Freshen up and then meet us downstairs. I'm ordering Chinese for dinner. I've had way too many fancy meals over the last couple of days and I'm starving."

Brandon stood and grabbed Nikolai's hand before he could turn away. "I love you. I'm glad you're here."

Nikolai's beamed a smile at Brandon, leaning in to kiss him gently. "I love you too. So much. Now, come on. We have family dinner then I hope to bribe Jeremy into reading Casey her story so I can take you to bed."

"Yeah? Jeremy is very bribable, as it turns out. Just offer to take him driving so he can get more practice in for his test."

"Oh, I like it. Thanks for the inside tip. Do as I said, get freshened up then come join us."

"Okay." Nikolai walked to the door, stopping to blow Brandon a kiss before opening it and closing it gently behind him.

Brandon shook himself out of his stupor when he realized he was staring at the closed door and he went back to the bathroom to wash his face and make himself presentable. He had a family dinner to attend.

* * * *

Three hours later and Brandon was finally alone with Nikolai again. Pressing Nikolai up against the wall, he kissed him hungrily. "You have been driving me crazy with all your touching tonight."

"Really?"

"Your innocent act does not fool me. You did it on purpose, you evil, evil man."

Nikolai burst into laughter. "It wasn't on purpose at first, but your reactions were way too much fun to not continue once I realized."

Brandon took another kiss, thrusting his tongue inside Nikolai's mouth and gently rocking his hips to get some friction on his erection. "It feels like I've been hard for hours. Oh, wait… That's because you're evil, and I have been hard for hours."

Nikolai reached up and grabbed the hair at the back of Brandon's head, giving it a yank and making Brandon moan. Nik leaned in and nipped at his exposed throat. "You're not complaining, are you, baby?"

"No. No. Please."

"Get undressed and on the bed. Hands and knees."

Brandon rushed to comply, glad he was only wearing a T-shirt, sweats and a jock at this point. He stripped everything off and threw it in the direction of the chair as he grabbed the lube out of the drawer, throwing it on top of the comforter and climbing on to the bed. Nikolai's groan was gratifying, and Brandon wiggled his ass to make sure he had his complete attention, hiding his face in his pillow so Nikolai wouldn't see his smile. He popped his head out of hiding when Nikolai slapped his ass while climbing up behind him. He couldn't have stopped the moan that came out if he'd tried.

"Oh, *dorogoy*. You liked that, didn't you?" Nikolai slapped the opposite butt cheek, and Brandon pushed his ass out for more. Nikolai started a steady rhythm of slaps, alternating between the two sides. He reached under Brandon and wrapped a warm hand around his aching cock. "You really like it. Something to explore in depth later. For now, I've missed you too much, and I need in your ass. The heat from your spanking will certainly add something to the experience for sure." Nikolai kneaded his left cheek for a moment with his other hand, making Brandon moan again, before the lube cap opened and a drizzle of cold liquid squirted onto the crevice of his ass and dripped into his hole, then a slick finger was added to the mix. Nikolai first circled his hole with the finger then slowly pressed for entry. Brandon did everything he could to relax.

"Please, Nik. I need you. I'm ready."

"No, you're not. You need at least two more fingers, babe. I won't hurt you." Nikolai started stroking Brandon and he worked himself between Nikolai's finger and the stroking hand. He whimpered gratefully when Nikolai added the second then third fingers.

"Please."

"You beg so nicely, *dorogoy*. You need me in every way, don't you? My perfect match."

Brandon was coming out of his skin. "Yes. Please. I need you. You're mine. I'm yours. Take me!"

"Sh-h. Easy." Nikolai lined up and started pushing in.

"Not slow. Please. I don't need slow."

Nikolai hesitated behind him. "Are you sure?"

"I'm sure. Please. Show me I belong to you."

Nikolai took a firmer grip of Brandon's hips and took Brandon at his word, taking him just how Brandon needed it—hard and fast, claiming.

"Yes! Yes! Like that!"

Nikolai let go of Brandon's hip with one hand and grabbed his shoulder instead. He began slamming into Brandon with every thrust, as he responded to Brandon's plea. "You are mine. Never forget. You are mine."

"Yours. Yes. Yours." Brandon wanted it to last forever, but he could feel the telltale tingle indicating his imminent orgasm.

"You need to come, *dorogoy*. Come *now*!"

The command sent Brandon hurtling over the edge. It was almost painful because it felt so good. He couldn't hold himself up any longer and collapsed to the bed, not caring that he was in the wet spot. When Nikolai went to pull out, Brandon reached behind him to stop Nikolai from moving. "Not yet. I need to feel you." Nikolai collapsed onto Brandon's back, giving him his weight. "Thank you. That's what I needed."

"Which? Me to crush you or me to fuck you stupid?"

Brandon huffed out a laugh. "Both, actually."

Nikolai's answering laugh had him pulling free of Brandon, making them both groan. Nikolai pressed a kiss below Brandon's ear before getting off the bed and going to the bathroom. Brandon distantly heard the water turn off and on several times, then Nikolai was back, cleaning him with a warm cloth. Brandon turned over onto his back, and Nik used the cloth to swipe at the mess on the comforter before tossing it in the direction of the hamper. Climbing under the covers and holding his arms out to Nikolai, Brandon sighed deeply when Nikolai climbed in and snuggled into him, putting his head on Brandon's chest.

"I love you, babe."

Nikolai's arms tightened around him for a moment. "I love you too."

"Welcome home."

Epilogue

Nikolai looked around at the crowd of people gathered for Sasha's college send-off party in the Hamiltons' backyard. All his favorite people were all in one place. Kirk and Eric's girls were playing with Casey in the pool. Jeremy was scoping out the food table with Jessie and Sasha. Strangely, Nikolai didn't see any of Sasha's other friends.

Nikolai was distracted from that thought by the sight of Grace sitting at the outdoor bar, showing off her engagement ring to anyone who happened to wander close. Nikolai was twenty feet away and he still had no problem seeing it. Her accountant fiancé, Jeff, sat silently next to her, letting her shine. They were perfect together.

Saul and Lee were talking to Kirk and Eric over by the grill. Sergei was the first to see Nikolai from where he and Stuart were in a couple of lounge chairs by the pool.

"Nikolai! Glad you made it! Brandon was getting worried."

Nikolai made his way over to him. "Yeah, I was worried too. I didn't think my flight from London was ever going to take off. It was delay after delay." Nikolai heard a commotion behind him and started to turn around until Stuart stood and snagged him into a hug.

Nikolai was so confused. Stuart didn't usually hug him. Stuart held him out at arms-length to talk to him. "It was a great honor for you to be asked to present another paper at that London conference, though. You had to go."

"I know. It's all good, and I made it. Have you seen my boyfriend, though? I can't seem to find him anywhere."

"Maybe."

Nikolai looked at Stuart in disbelief. "What do you mean 'maybe'?"

Stuart put his hands on Nikolai's shoulders and turned him around. On the deck leading out to the pool, Sasha, Jeremy, Jessie and Casey were each standing holding a sign with one word per sign. *Will. You. Marry. Me.* At the end of the line was Brandon on one knee holding out a box with a ring in it.

Nikolai brought his hands to his mouth, and he walked in slow-motion until he was standing in front of his boyfriend, where Brandon took hold of his left hand.

"Nik, I love you. You're already a part of our family, but will you make it official and please marry me?"

"Yes. Of course, yes. Absolutely yes. I love you so much."

Brandon slid the ring onto his finger and stood, pulling Nik close to kiss him breathless. The applause distantly registered, and Nik pulled away. "Did everyone know about this?"

"Yep. I've been planning it for weeks. This is our engagement party. Sasha was kind enough to let us pretend this was his going-away party to get you here. I was stressing when your flight kept being delayed."

"You didn't think I would say no, did you?"

"No, but you had to be here for it."

"True. I love you."

"Love you too."

Then Casey was wrapped around their legs. "I love you, too, Papa."

Nik leaned down to scoop her up, aware that she was wet and likely ruining his suit. But he didn't care. "I am so lucky to be part of this family. I can't wait to make it official. Bring it in, Jeremy. Family hug." Of course, it wasn't only Jeremy who came, as Nik found himself surrounded on all sides by everyone there.

Blood, found and made. It all came down to one word...family.

Want to see more from this author? Here's a taster for you to enjoy!

Kingdom of Corazón: The Way to a Man's Heart
Ann Marie James

Excerpt

The royal family of the Kingdom of Corazón greeted their guests for the Midsummers Ball as Christian watched. He ran a hand down the front of his dress military uniform to straighten it while he waited for his turn to be announced. This was his first formal duty as the newly appointed Royal Military Liaison, and he needed to make sure he looked his best. He shifted his feet to find some relief for his ankle, which was still sore from him standing for a long time. His last mission had not gone to plan, and a broken ankle had been the result. Although the cast had come off a couple of weeks prior, it still wasn't one hundred percent.

"Royal Military Liaison Lieutenant Diaz," the herald announced. Christian caught the eye of Crown Prince Sebastian toward the end of the greeting line and his best friend's eyes widened in surprise before his face lit up with happiness at seeing him. As the only child of the Castle Commander, Christian had grown up here, but he'd been in the service away from the castle for ten years. At thirty, Christian was the same age as Crown Prince Sebastian. They had been best friends from the time they had been in diapers, and even though Christian and the prince still got together when their schedules allowed, it wasn't the same as seeing and being with him every day. Christian had missed him fiercely.

The royal children of the kingdom were usually paired with a young playmate from the age of about ten. Christian had started earlier than age ten as Sebastian's companion, since he was always with him anyway. As Castle Commander, his father was the head of the guard slash castle security. He'd taken the companion idea a step further and trained Christian to be as good as he could be in martial arts and marksmanship. In his father's eyes, Christian was to act as another line of defense for the Crown Prince. While Christian had not carried a gun—that was the role of the actual bodyguards—he was trained in case he ever had to use one.

With a nod to the herald, Christian stepped forward to greet the Queen of the Kingdom of Corazón. Queen Tania reached out both hands to Christian, and he clasped them and raised them to his lips while bowing over them. "My Queen… It is a pleasure to see you. You haven't changed a bit."

"Lieutenant Diaz, it is a pleasure to see you as well. Ten years is way too long. We have missed you."

"I apologize for the lengthy absence, Your Highness. I needed a change, but I am assigned here for the foreseeable future, so you will have time to get sick of me again."

"So my husband has told me. I am excited to have you home, although in a different capacity as the Royal Military Liaison. I look forward to catching up."

"As do I."

The queen turned a stern eye on her eldest daughter, who was standing to her right. "Princess Zia, isn't it wonderful that Christian will be back with us for a while?"

Christian tried to mask his sneer as his gaze went to Zia, who was not at all happy this evening. Of course, she wouldn't be, since she wasn't the center of attention. She wasn't a very nice person and never had been. She was also part of the reason he'd left and joined the military. *What she did...* No, he wasn't going to think about it. It was in the past. He was stronger and even more deadly now. It was time for him to face his demons. The military had finished the training his father had started, turning him into a true weapon. At twenty-eight, Christian had hoped Zia would have grown up and stopped being so self-absorbed, but the affliction seemed to have gotten worse instead of better in the time Christian had been away.

Christian gave Princess Zia a shallow bow. "Princess Zia." That was all he could manage. He wasn't going to lie and say he'd missed her.

Princess Zia tossed back her hair and gave him her haughtiest look. "Mr. Diaz."

"It's Lieutenant Diaz, actually, Your Highness." Christian didn't wait for her to respond, instead turning to greet the king of the Kingdom of Corazón. A striking man, even in his fifties, King Raul Hart exuded a sense of calm authority that Christian had always admired, making him seem larger than life. "King Raul." Christian bowed low in front of the man. When he straightened, Christian was shocked to realize that he was now taller than the king. When they had met briefly the day before, the king had been busy on a phone call and had just waved him into his office and into a chair. Christian had experienced another surprise growth spurt after he had joined the military at age twenty and was now six-three, but he hadn't realized that made him taller than the king.

"Hello again, Royal Military Liaison Lieutenant Diaz." The king's eyes twinkled at him as he ignored protocol and pulled Christian into a hug. "I didn't get a chance to do that when we met yesterday. I wanted to correct that error."

"Yes, sir." Christian returned the hug before stepping back and offering him a crisp salute. "Lieutenant Diaz reporting for duty, sir."

"As you were, Lieutenant. Now I think there's someone here who can't wait to greet you. It was hard keeping this a secret from him."

"I know. I talked to him earlier, and I almost spilled the beans."

Christian moved down the line and tried to keep a stern expression on his face as he saluted before grinning at one of his best friends. "Crown Prince."

"Why didn't you tell me you were being assigned to the castle as Royal Military Liaison?"

"I thought you would like the surprise of it. It just happened a few days ago." Christian once more ran a hand down the front of his military uniform. "First mission, the Midsummer's Ball. It's a very tough assignment."

"Well, I'm glad you're here. I can't wait to see more of you, and as a bonus, now I won't have to drive to visit you."

Christian scoffed. "Like it's that far to the base or my house from here."

"When I was used to you being always at my side, it's too far."

"It's been ten years, Bas."

"Too far. Too long."

"Yes, Your Highness." Christian couldn't help the eye roll at the end. It was good to be back with friends.

Prince Sebastian just grinned in response.

"My turn. My turn."

Christian turned his head to the left to see Princess Katarina waving him down the line. "Princess Katarina, it is a pleasure to see you again."

"I am so excited you made it and that we will get to see more of you."

"Me too, Your Highness."

He leaned forward to kiss her cheek and she took the opportunity to whisper in his ear.

"I think you have broken our Head Chef."

"What?" Christian pulled back so he could look in her eyes, as if that would somehow make what she'd said make sense.

"He is standing over by the hors d'oeuvres table and has been staring at you since you were announced." Katarina giggled. "He looks like someone has struck him."

Christian shook his head at her, although his heart sped up at the thought of seeing his old crush, but he tried not to show that her words had affected him. "I will leave you to greet the rest of your guests. We can catch up later."

"Save me a dance, please, Lieutenant."

"It would be an honor, Princess."

Christian glanced over at the hors d'oeuvre table to find Max Ramirez indeed staring at him. The eye contact must have startled him because he jumped then looked at his shoes for a moment and clasped his hands behind his back. Christian strode across the room to greet him, determined not to make an ass of himself. He pulled Max into a quick hug in greeting, before holding him out at arm's length so he could get a better look at him.

Max had been his older teenage crush and was the epitome of everything he had ever dreamed of in a man. *I obviously still have it bad for the guy.* At six-foot-five, Max was a giant—but a gentle one. Christian was still leaner than Max, but along with the growth spurt, he had put on a lot of muscle and his frame had filled out a lot since the last time they had seen each other, making them more equal in stature. There was something about the man that had always called to him.

"Max! How are you doing?"

"I'm doing great. Head Chef now."

"I heard. Six years ago now, right? Everyone was talking about you being the youngest to ever get the job."

"Yeah. They told me on my thirtieth birthday. I did *not* see it coming." Max had started as an apprentice to the head chef, Howie Klein, straight out of culinary school. The twenty-year-old had met the chef's cranky, militaristic style in the kitchen with a smile on his face. Which, as the last apprentice had stormed out of the kitchen after throwing a pan at Mr. Klein's head, had been important.

"Yeah. It's too bad about the arthritis in Mr. Klein's feet. I still talk to his son Ryan frequently. He told me his father was gutted to have to retire but happy to have you to move into the position. Good for you. It was a well-earned promotion."

"He still stops in from time to time to give his opinion on things, so I still get to see him. Thank you. I'm proud of their faith in me. I'm assuming this is a promotion for you?"

"Yep. Going to be assigned to the castle for a while." There was an awkward pause in the conversation. Christian turned so he was standing shoulder to shoulder with Max and could have a better view of the room. He waved a hand indicating the greeting line. "I can't believe Princess Katarina is eighteen already."

"Right? She was, what? Eight when you left? She seemed pleased to see you. I'm surprised she remembered you."

"I was assigned to be her personal guard when she visited colleges last summer. We spent eight weeks together. We got to know each other pretty well."

"Oh. No one said. What about Prince Sebastian?"

"We still hang out and talk as often as we can. I inherited my grandmother's cottage on the west side of the island. Sebastian usually visits me there when I'm on-island."

"What about Ryan? You said you still talk to him frequently?"

"I still consider him one of my best friends, along with Prince Sebastian." Christian laughed self-deprecatingly. "We bonded over our unrequited crushes. His on Prince Sebastian and mine on you." He gave Max a quick wink before turning his attention back to the room. "I visit him as often as I can in Boston, and we try to talk at least once a week, when possible. He'll be here tonight, actually, along with his best friend from college and her husband."

"He will?"

"Yep. Princess Katarina insisted. We stayed with Ryan while touring colleges in Boston, and she got to know all of them."

"Ryan is almost a full-fledged doctor now, right?"

"He's actually done already. Four years as an undergrad at Harvard, then four years of medical school. He finished up his residency a few weeks ago. Speaking of…" Christian elbowed Max in the side, ignoring the tingle where they touched, and nodded toward the entry. Christian made sure to be watching Prince Sebastian's expression, when first the Surgeon General of the Island, Doctor Guttschein, was announced, then Ryan Klein was there with his friends Emma and Ian Robinson.

"Wow. He's definitely grown up." Max chuckled. "The prince obviously thinks so too."

He couldn't help but chuckle as he watched Sebastian's jaw drop in astonishment. Ryan had changed a lot over the years, going from gangly and coltish to becoming a well-proportioned hunk. *Yep. He's just Sebastian's type now.* He followed Ryan and his friends with his gaze as they made their way through the greeting line, chuckling to himself as he noted Sebastian's impatience as he waited for his turn to speak to Ryan.

Princess Katarina waved a hand in Christian and Max's direction as she finished greeting them. Ryan's face lit up as he saw them, and he hurried over to embrace Max after shooting Christian a grin.

"You are certainly a sight for sore eyes, Ryan."

"Thanks, Max. It's great to see you."

"Gah." Max slapped Ryan on the back then gave him an assessing look. "You are way too thin. We need to work on fattening you up a bit."

"I was busy learning. Didn't have much time for cooking. Let me introduce you to my friends from America. Emily and Ian, this is the chef you heard me going on about. Emily is also a doctor in the Island Doctor program and will be working with me here on Corazón. Ian is her husband and a very talented carpenter. Ian did his best to keep us fed, but sometimes it was a decision between sleep or eating," Ryan finished with a shrug.

"It is an honor to meet you, sir." Ian extended his hand for a shake. "This one" — with a thumb point back to Ryan — "talked about yours and his dad's cooking all the time. Memories of food and the kitchen were like his happy place when he was particularly stressed."

Ryan grinned widely at Ian's comment but didn't deny it. "The kitchen was my happy place. Max did a great job of making sure there was always something available for Christian, Prince Sebastian and me during those starving teenage years."

"Yes, I couldn't wait to meet you. I feel like I know you already." Emily stepped up and hugged Max instead of shaking his hand.

Max looked shocked for a moment but gently hugged her back. "It is great to meet you as well."

"Christian," Emily gushed, "how are you? Ian has missed you."

"I did." Ian nodded. "It's great when I have someone to talk to about something non-medical related or who isn't zombie-level tired."

"Yes, dear, I know we have treated you so badly." Emily patted his cheek in a condescending but loving manner before turning back to Christian. "Anyway, all that's behind us. Ryan and I start at the hospital in August. They are giving us a few weeks to settle in and reset."

"I look forward to hanging out with all of you. You're staying with Ryan in his cottage, right?"

"Just for a short time. Surprise! We bought the cottage on the other side of Ryan from you."

"Really? The Svenson place? I heard Mrs. Svenson passed away a couple of months ago but didn't even think about it."

"Yep. We bought it. It needs a lot of updating, though."

Christian cringed thinking about the last time he had seen inside the very dated house. "I remember the avocado appliances."

"Yeah, but it's all ours."

"Can't wait."

"How's the ankle? Glad to see you are out of the cast."

"What happened to your ankle?"

Christian looked at Max in surprise when he heard the note of panic in his voice. "I broke it about eight weeks ago on my last mission. Just got out of the cast a few weeks ago, so it's light duty for a few more weeks until I can finish the physical therapy. Should be good as new after that." Christian held his foot out and rotated it in a circle to show it was fine.

"Why didn't you let me know? I could have come to help—or at least sent food, wherever you were. I'm assuming you were here on the island for at least part of your recovery."

"Why would I have called for help? It's just an ankle. I've had worse."

A look of shock crossed Max's face. "When were you hurt worse?"

Christian gave another one-shouldered shrug. "It comes with the job, Max. You know that."

They were interrupted by the arrival of Christian's father before the discussion could go any further.

"Christian. Ryan." No hug. No smile. Just their names and a head nod. "I heard you were back."

"Yes, sir. On light duty for a few more weeks, but the powers-that-be thought it would be good for me to represent them at this shindig." Christian waved a hand to encompass the ballroom and all the people as he finished speaking. If Christian had expected the great Juan Diaz, head of the royal guard, to be happy to see him—which he hadn't—he would have been hurt by his father's reaction.

"Huh. And here I thought you'd actually smartened up and were ready to come back full-time and accept your responsibilities here."

"I *am* coming back to accept my responsibilities here. I'm a lieutenant in this country's army and I am doing my duty as assigned."

"Don't take that tone with me, young man."

"I'm not, sir." Christian squared his shoulders and faced his father, looking him directly in the eye and lowering his voice so the other people around them wouldn't hear. "I am living my life the way I want to—not *your* plan for my life…mine. Now, if you'll excuse me. I have some appetizers to eat and friends to catch up with. I'll let you get back to your *duties*." Christian made sure to put as much emphasis on the word 'duties' as he could.

He had heard enough lectures growing up about the importance of performing his duties—how he had to be at his best at all times, how he had to be *serious*. There had been no time for play in the Diaz household.

Juan Diaz' only reaction was a clenched jaw. Christian swore he could almost hear his father's teeth creak from the pressure. Without another word, Juan turned on his heel and strode away.

Christian closed his eyes while pinching the bridge of his nose for a moment to get his emotions under control. He'd done it. He'd stood up to his father. Ryan wrapped his arm around Christian's waist and gave him a side hug.

"Good job," he whispered.

"Thanks," he whispered back. "Why are we whispering?"

Ryan squeezed him again. "Because I know you don't know how to take a compliment. Not sure if he actually heard you, but you said what you've been wanting to say, so that's good."

Christian wrapped his arm around Ryan's waist and gave him a quick squeeze in return before raising his voice to normal levels. "Yeah. Well, let's forget about it for now and focus on the wonderful food Max and his crew have made for the ball." He turned toward the chef. "You have truly outdone yourself, Max."

"You know I love to do stuff like this. It's been a blast working with Katarina. I love the tradition where the royal gets to plan the Midsummer's Ball as their first adult event-planning after they turn eighteen. I think everyone is really going to enjoy everything she has come up with for this event."

"I don't think that's what my father said when he was working with Princess Zia when it was her turn," Ryan said dryly.

"Well, Zia's event was a bit different. She wanted to make hers an exclusive event only for certain people, and that was her choice of how to use her budget. Katarina has been more about including as many people as possible. It's been great to see her operate. She is well-loved—and look at how great everything is."

Everyone turned to inspect how the room was decorated for the event. Princess Katarina had gone with a fairy garden party theme. Flowers in a rainbow of colors were distributed throughout the room, with small, twisted grapevine sculptures of different fairies sitting on beds of petals serving as the centerpieces. Christian was especially impressed by the artistry of the Fairy King and Queen ice sculpture over by the drinks table. The whole effect was warm and yet classy. The doors were open to the outside, where the garden was decorated with lights, and more grapevine sculptures were hidden in the branches of the bushes and trees.

Christian chuckled. "As I told you, I can't believe she's eighteen already and doing stuff like this. It doesn't seem that long ago that I was feeding her a bottle and changing her diaper."

Ryan scoffed. "If memory serves me correctly, you avoided diaper issues at all costs."

"Only because I had very important duties to handle with the prince."

"Uh-huh. Like sneaking out to go for ice cream?"

"We only did that once!" Christian's feigned outrage made Ryan laugh, which had been his intention.

Ryan reached out and cupped Christian's neck. "I'm glad you're here right now. I've missed you. Hopefully now that I've moved here permanently, we will be able to hang out more."

"We will. I only have a few months left on this enlistment. I'm not sure if I'm going to re-sign or not. Don't know what I would do next, but I think I'm ready for something new. Right now, I've actually been reassigned as the liaison to the castle for the foreseeable future."

"Wait. You're going to be around more?" Ryan sounded truly pleased with the idea.

"Yep. Anyway"—Christian rubbed his hands together while looking over the food on the tables—"I'm starving. I know the dinner isn't for another hour, so let's dig in. I have definitely missed Max's cooking."

Max grinned at all of them. "I look forward to having you all around, both old friends and new. I have missed the two of you. Now, I must get back to my kitchen. Who knows what crisis is lurking?" With a wave, Max turned and disappeared through the door leading into his domain.

Christian couldn't help watching Max's ass as he walked away, only to be interrupted by Ryan clapping him on the back. "You've still got it bad, man."

"Like you can talk," Ian said as he threw his arm over his wife's shoulders. "Did you see him drooling over the prince?"

"I did. I also saw the prince doing his own drooling."

"I can't deny it. Prince Sebastian is still very fine."

"Agreed," Christian said. "Now to put operation *Come to Daddy* in action."

"For the last time, we are *not* calling it that."

"*Operation Nookie Time*?"

"No." Ryan gave Christian a shove. "Let's just get some food, dork."

Christian laughed as he grabbed a plate and started loading it up with a little bit of everything…except the fish. Christian hated fish in any form. Always had. Max had tried for years to find a fish dish he liked. As they were an island country, that made it difficult for him sometimes. Luckily, the island also had sheep, poultry, some beef and he was okay with different kinds of seafood, but not fish.

Christian and Ryan talked and joked with everyone in the group, in between speaking to all the people who came up to welcome them home. Ryan introduced Emily and Ian as they talked and everyone made sure they both were included in the conversations as much as possible. Ryan snagged the hand of a sneak thief trying to steal a shrimp from his plate.

"Sorry, Your Highness," Ryan quickly released Sebastian's wrist, when he realized who it was. "You do know there's a ton of food right there, don't you?" Ryan pointed at the still-full tables of appetizers.

"Yep, but stolen treats taste better. It's been scientifically proven."

"Has it now?" Ryan queried dryly. "And where can I find the results of this scientific study?"

"It's well known. You can find it anywhere," the prince responded.

"Uh-huh."

"Whew," Emily interrupted fanning herself with her hand. "Is it getting hot in here or is just me?"

Christian shook his head in mock disgust. "The two of them have always been that way. Although it's nice to see that the prince finally bought a clue and understood what is right in front of him."

The prince whipped his head around so he could stare at his long-time friend. "What?"

"What? Ryan is one of the few people who can challenge you intellectually and keep up with you physically as far as training. I am one of the others, but there has never been any chemistry between the two of us. The two of you, on the other hand? You start talking and it's like the rest of the world ceases to exist."

"Really?" Ryan said. "That's interesting to hear. I always thought my crush on the prince was hopeless. In fact, I believe the prince even told me he didn't see me as anything but a friend."

Christian pretended to lower his voice and spoke in a stage whisper. "Plot twist, spoiler alert. He lied." Christian switched his voice to normal. "Especially now that Ryan has grown into" — Christian paused to wave a hand in Ryan's direction, indicating his body from top to bottom — "all this. Ryan is everything Sebastian ever said he wanted." Christian watched with amusement as the prince squirmed.

"Not to change the subject or anything, but what are you doing here? You didn't tell me you were coming to the ball." Prince Sebastian stepped forward and pulled Christian into a quick guy-clench.

His friend's laughter and joking eased something inside Christian. *Man, it's good to be home.*

PUBLISHING

Sign up for our newsletter and find out about all our romance book releases, eBook sales and promotions, sneak peeks and FREE romance books!

About the Author

Ann Marie James is fluent in two languages, English and sarcasm. She believes that you will never learn anything new if you don't read as much as you can, and/or talk to every stranger you meet. She always looks for the best in people and to treat people the way she wants to be treated. Above all Ann Marie believes in love, whatever form it takes. Relationships are hard, love is the glue that keeps it together.

Ann Marie loves to hear from readers. You can find her contact information, website details and author profile page at https://www.pride-publishing.com